Table of Contents

Praise for Melanie James

A Valentine's Surprise - "It was one of the cutest and hottest novellas I've ever read. It's rare to have such a great mix of cute and hot, but this author does it perfectly!" ~ Willow Star Serenity Reviews

A Valentine's Surprise - "This is one of the best short stories I have read in a long time!" ~ HeadTripping Books

A Valentine's Surprise - "This little love story is capable of getting your juices going and turning a dull afternoon into a page turning glorious day." ~ Aubree Lane, Author of Sierra Mist & Early One Morning"

Conjuring Darkness - "I was already a huge fan of author Melanie James so I expected her to write another amazing book. Even I didn't expect how incredible Conjuring Darkness would be. I couldn't put it down!" ~ Kelly Cozzone, Author of Tropical Dreams

A Valentine's Surprise - "Kuddos to Melanie James for throwing a good romance our way. I want more!" ~ Jennifer Theriot, Author, Out Of the Box Series

Conjuring Darkness – "Conjuring Darkness captivates your attention right from the start and never let's go. The adventure packed into this supernatural thriller only keeps you on the edge and turning the page. It definitely was one of those books that was hard to put down." ~ Angela Ford, Author of Closure

Conjuring Darkness – *"This book is captivating from the first page, I could not put the book down. I was so surprised by all the twists, turns, the unexpected. I could not wait until I was through each chapter." ~ Angie at I Heart Books*

Hot reads by Melanie James

Seasons of Love Series

A Valentine's Surprise

A Summer Love – July 2014

Fall in Love – Coming fall 2014

Literal Leigh Romance Diaries

Accidental Leigh

Serious Leigh – Coming Soon

Stand Alone

Beautiful Betrayals – Coming August 2014

Darkness Series

Conjuring Darkness

Hour of Darkness – Fall 2014

Edition License Notes

Copyright

Accidental Leigh

By Melanie James

Copyright © by Melanie James

Editing: Black Paw Publishing

Proofreading: AVCProofreading

Cover Artist: Dreams to Media

ISBN-13:
978-1499232509

ISBN-10:
1499232500

Acknowledgements

To my amazing assistant Stephanie Mae. There are not enough words to express how grateful I am to have met you! Your support means the world to me and I am always in awe of your hard work!

Monkeys – Thank you so much for everything. You all are amazing! My tree would be awfully lonely without each and every one of you to fill it up!

CLS – Rock on! #PTTP!

Thank you to all of my readers for the continued support. You have given me more than you know!

Dedication

This book is for my amazing kids. I couldn't imagine life without the five of you!

Chapter One

Goodbye Carl, Hello Vlad!

Apparently, the strangest, yet most powerful thing has happened to me, which isn't saying much. After all, I'm a single, overworked and under-fucked elementary school teacher. This strange and magical thing wasn't expected and I sort of stumbled on it by accident.

Maybe, I should first explain what led up to this discovery. Let's just say that because I have a non-existent love life, I've decided to spend my summer break doing something new. I decided to write romance stories. Like most women, I love reading romance books that are unabashedly hot. Let's call it my guilty pleasure. Don't get me wrong, I read a lot. I get into the brainy essays and the trending book club recommendations. I love the classics as well. Reading has been the single most influential part of my life, but nothing gets the juices flowing quite like a steamy, smoking hot hero who delivers orgasm after panty wetting orgasm.

Some (mostly men) would sneer at the way women consume romance books. I've heard men refer to romance books as nothing but pulp. They like to call them bodice rippers, mommy porn, paperback porn, and the like. Women, and a growing number of romance reading men, would agree with me when I say the romance genre of today is a rich source of good fiction that really draws from so much more. Is it full of erotica? Hell yes! Is it full of feel-good Happily Ever Afters? Sometimes. Let's face it. Women are smart readers. They know what they want and what they need. Maybe some of the Nay-Sayers (mostly men) could learn a little bit about how to be a real man from a good fictional alpha male. God knows, the male gender seems to be sorely lacking in some of those qualities these days. Hence, we have to get what we need and what we want from fiction.

To say the least, I'm a book-whore and I follow multiple series and authors. You had better believe, I keep my masturbatory fantasies pretty stocked up with just about anything that could possibly suit my mood. I have a pretty creative imagination that often puts together some exciting ideas. All of my naughty ideas are drawn from the themes from my reading habit. In the past year, I realized that I had developed a true artistic vision, and I pondered what I could do with my creativity. Why not write these stories down? They could someday be bestsellers! Like I said, something strange happened and that is why I need to keep a diary of what's going on.

It all started last fall. I had been casually dating a guy named Carl, a math teacher at the middle school. Don't get me wrong, he's a nice guy. He just doesn't come close to being a shadow of what my book boyfriends are like, and he could never even dream of being the lead hero in anyone's fictional fantasy, let alone mine. Carl is just too… dare I say, bland. He's soft, pale, and a little lumpy.

I have a category for guys that fit this exact description. Marshmallows. Marshmallows have some good qualities though, they can't simply be overlooked. They are usually decent guys that are financially stable. They just don't have what it takes to get the juices flowing, if you know what I mean. Carl never gave me that initial jolt that made me even consider having sex with him. The passion never even smoldered. Hell, who am I kidding, the spark never ignited!

One Saturday morning, he called and wanted to see if I'd like to go out to dinner and catch a movie. I really tried to ignore him, but he's a persistent little bugger. I found myself scrambling for ways that I could be tactful about saying, I already had plans. I mean, it was the day that I had been eagerly awaiting for months. I had finished reading the third book in the Shifted Hearts Vampiric Wolf series the day after it was released. This next installment promised to be hot, and I was foaming at the mouth!

Book four was ready and willing to provide the long awaited pleasure that I so desperately needed. I was all set. I had bought the perfect mood candles, the bath soaps, and a giant size pack of AA batteries. We're not talking about the family size package, no, no, no... This was the size that the Red Cross orders during extended power outages resulting from catastrophic natural disasters. I hate to admit this, but I even bought the perfect skimpy little negligée to wear after my four hour bath. Oh hell, I might as well admit it, I had already received a special gift to myself. It arrived in discreet, plain brown packaging. The gift promised to measure up to Vladimir Wolf's fictional hardened length, every long, thick inch of it. Where was I? Oh yeah. Back to Carl, who couldn't let go. I finally let it blurt out of my mouth.

"Carl! I told you that I already have plans. I'm busy tonight."

"Doing what, Leigh?"

"Dammit! I have a date already!"

"Oh? Really? With *who*?" Carl said *who* with a very nasally and sarcastic tone, by the way, and that really just pissed me right the fuck off! We're talking about my boy Vlad, now. Nobody and I mean nobody talks bad about Vlad!

"You wouldn't know him, his name is Vladimir, and he's from Romania."

"What? Let me guess, you have a date with another one of your fictional characters. That's what it sounds like to me. Leigh, why didn't you just say you didn't want to see me anymore?"

"OK fine, Carl. I would rather stay at home and masturbate than go out with you!" The stinging words rolled off of my tongue and hung in the atmosphere between cell phone towers like a swarm of angry bees. I clamped my mouth shut, as if I could still stop them from getting to Carl, but it was too late.

I had everything just right. The mood was set and I slipped into a nice warm bath with my Kindle ready for action. Then it happened. In the second chapter, my beloved Vladimir, my hero, my fantasy love, was dead. Dead! Some low-life werewolves killed my vampire-wolf shifter with a wooden stake wrapped in silver. I screamed in pure agony, "Dead? Dead! No!" I spent the next couple of hours sitting on my bed crying, my tears dropping on my Kindle. Sad, I know. I called my sister in Pittsburgh, who shared my love for Vlad. I needed support and she sadly couldn't offer it. All we did was cry over the untimely passing of our beloved Vladimir, and make threats against the writer who swiftly brought grief into our lives. All the while, my mood candles pathetically melted away, alone.

As the weeks went by, I slogged my way through the stages of grief over that damn book. It was a very serious thing for me. I was officially in mourning. I subconsciously chose black to wear to work. Who does that sort of thing? Me, that's who! It didn't go unnoticed by the other teachers, or even the students at my school. The day I realized that my grief was on full display was when a small voice asked. "Miss Epstein? Did somebody croak or something?" I lost it again. "Croak?" I couldn't tell the little girl the truth. "Yes, Haley, someone did, in fact, croak. Somebody very dear to me. My boyfriend." Kids! They are very observant, but they can be such uncouth little mongrels. I felt awful for lying, not because I was lying to a child, no. I only felt awful because I knew that I had just cast out the first of many threads which would eventually be woven into a huge web of deceit.

As the weeks went by, that little lie spread through the class like an infestation of head lice. Then the lie reached up from the sticky mass of mucus that is the student body and spread to the teachers' lounge. Nothing gives the lunchroom coterie of stressed out teachers the dark and secret joy of morose delectation like good gossip. Like any viral lie, the croaking of Leigh's boyfriend had grown. It became altered into a story of fantastic proportions. I felt the gravity of the lie, when finally, one of the perky new teachers approached me.

"Leigh, I just want to tell you that I am very sorry for your loss."

I was caught a bit off guard and had to scramble to recover so I didn't blow it. "Huh? Oh, thanks."

"I lost my great-aunt a few years ago and it affected me deeply. I just can't imagine losing my entire family in such a tragedy."

I was curious now to know what the hell kind of tragedy had taken out my entire family. I wanted to lead her on, but I wasn't quite sure of how to do it. "Yes. Yes, it was."

She handed me a large folded poster board. "One of my students had asked if the entire first grade class could make a sympathy card for you. I hope you don't mind the graphic images, but I believe the children should be allowed to freely express their feelings. I think it cultivates their empathy. Don't you agree? I was just reading a study-"

My stomach churned at her still fresh first year teacher peppiness. She handed me the card that was adorned with a few doodles of what appeared to be bananas flying out of a box. Scattered around were dismembered stick figures with X's for eyes.

"Oh my God!" I interrupted her discussion on the relationship between creative expression and empathy with my shock at seeing the grotesque artwork.

"What is it? I didn't mean to upset you."

"Oh… Sorry, it was just unexpected. What exactly does this show? I mean, are those bananas flying through the air?"

"No, those are fingers, except for those two. Those are severed penises. Oh, and I think those over here are bratwurst. That tiny addition was little Carter's contribution. Everyone heard how bad it was when the sausage plant exploded and your family's car was caught in a giant fireball."

I was trying with all of my might to keep from vomiting. "OK, well, tell them how much I appreciate their consoling thoughts."

I really wanted to ask her if she was secretly trying to groom the next generation of serial killers. I bit my tongue because more than wanting that question answered, I just wanted her to take her happy ass back to the classroom and leave me the hell alone. A sausage plant explosion was how my one tiny lie ended up? I supposed the gruesome details included a deluge of body parts and ground pork spattering the neighborhood. I imagined the surreal scene with empty sausage casings dangling from car antennas like so many discarded condoms.

I had no doubt, I had become the most recent fodder for discussion among my peers. I guess it must have been welcome. The other recent gossip included a middle school teacher's husband, Ron. He taught history at the high school, but was forced to make an unexpected exit after the dressing down of his entire class. Apparently, a student questioned whether it was relevant to learn about the French revolution. He told the entire class they needed to learn it or become a generation of stupid assholes, just like their stupid asshole parents who lived in a town full of assholes, dipshits, and dumbasses. He then went on to recite a list of the worst assholes by name, which happened to include the entire school board. Now, the only time we saw him around school was when he was dropping off something for his wife. If you said hello, he only grumbled, "Asshole" and turned away.

In any case, a certain degree of mourning was appropriate. As insane as it may seem to some, any true fan of a good romance series will validate my grief. You really have a tremendous amount of emotional investment with the book boyfriend. Maybe more than you would with the real-life boyfriend. Let's face it, when you are in the dating scene, you have a built-in level of expected disappointment. How many times have you heard it from your friends? You know, the "disclaimer." Those usually start out with, "Well, at least he can hold down a job." "Sure, he's no Chris Hemsworth, but at least he doesn't live in his parent's basement." And sometimes they get downright desperate. "Well, at least he didn't have to blow into a tube to start his car." The worse one I've heard someone say about their boyfriend was "you can barely notice the ankle monitoring bracelet."

In the series you are reading, you have an immortal, consistent, and perfect lover. You don't have to make excuses or apologize for him, like you would with the real-life boyfriend. The book boyfriend fills those empty spaces of your heart that most guys could never reach, and that's just the emotional side of it. I don't even want to mention the physical aspects.

Chapter Two

An Old Desk and a Shocking Experience

I finally shook off my obsessive disappointment with the author and channeled my bitterness into creative energy. I made a decision. I would take matters into my own hands and start to write my own books. Just to have *a plan* was refreshing. I looked forward to getting started.

One wintery day over my holiday break, I decided, as long as I had some free time, I would start preparing. Now, everyone knows that a writer has to have a little nook or cave where all of their creative ideas can get put into words. I have a one bedroom apartment that has whatever space my damn cat allows me to use for myself, which isn't much. First, I needed a desk. It's the one thing every writer needs, and I finally found one for free on the local online classifieds. Someone was getting rid of it and I immediately called the number.

"Hello?" It was an elderly woman that seemed sweet. I could just imagine the serene grandmother pausing her daily baking of fresh chocolate chip cookies to answer my inquisitive call.

"Hi, I'm calling about the desk you listed. What can you tell me about it?"

"It's a desk, not a job offer."

"OK. What's it made out of? Is it big or small? Can't you describe it a little?"

"It's small, wooden, and very old, and I want it gone. Do you want it or not?"

So much for the sweet, serene grandmother.

Of course, I said yes and by that afternoon, I stopped by the address. The home was an old run-down Victorian house in a run-down neighborhood. The desk was sitting out on the porch with a little sign that said FREE. The desk was very small and very old, just as the lady said over the phone. It was made from wood and finished with a dark reddish stain. It was nothing more than four table legs and a square top that lifted open to keep a few things inside. There was a drawer on the underside that pulled out. I guess you could say it is more of an antique secretary's desk because it was pretty small, at least smaller than I would imagine for an antique desk. Just big enough to use for a writing surface. Perfect for me, because I wouldn't have to deal with having an argument with my cat over moving her carpeted towers and tunnels.

I knocked on the door so that I could at least thank the lady, but nobody answered. Maybe that wasn't such a bad thing. I couldn't imagine the lady being any nicer in person than she was on the phone.

Once I loaded it into the trunk of my car, I looked back at the house and caught a brief glimpse of someone watching me from an upstairs window. The curtain was yanked quickly closed and although it was strange to me, I was happy to have found my little desk.

I made a nice little writing nook in my apartment. I placed the desk in the appropriate spot so that I would be able to look out the window. I imagined myself lost in fantasy, hammering out one best-seller after another. I had fun setting up my work space with as much inspirational décor as possible. You know, the girly stuff you pick up at any bookstore or gift shop. The sad thing was, that's where it all stayed, untouched until the end of the school year. Well, not exactly. My furry black cat, Luna, decided I had extended her playground by adding a nice little perch under the window. It also provided her with yet another set of scratching posts for sharpening her claws. Still, she scowled at me. My cat scowls, she can be such a bitch!

Now my summer break had arrived and I started on my characters. I needed to continue the theme of what I was reading, with a twist. Payback against werewolves. Any aspiring writer will probably tell you the same thing, names are hard to come up with. The werewolf I was writing about needed something, but since nothing came to mind, I just used Harry as a temporary name. It was one that would be easy to go back and change. I would assume most werewolves are somewhat hairy and Harry seemed as good as anything else at the time. I wanted him to fall madly in love with Beatrice, who happens to be the name of the author that killed my beloved Vlad. I had every intention of putting both of those characters through hell, eventually.

My first evening of writing was going to be fun. My muse, a bottle of chardonnay, plied me with a heavy hand toward the erotic. My fingers tickled my keyboard and a very naughty story glided across the monitor. It's one thing to read something titillating and erotic and quite another thing to actually write it. As a writer, you are dead certain as soon as you explore your kinkiest fantasies in a book, everyone in your life is going to find out that you wrote it. That is exactly the reason for the chardonnay and plenty of it. On that fateful night, the chardonnay won out against my inhibition. When I stopped, I left a chapter of my very erotic paranormal romance story to simmer for a day or two.

Sunday morning, I woke up to a very disturbing phone call. Any time my mother calls, it is most likely disturbing, but this time it was bad... really bad!

"Hi, Mom." I'm sure that I sounded flat and tired.

"Hello, Leigh. I just wanted to let you know that your father is in the hospital."

"Daddy? My God, what happened?" I was instantly thrown into shock. I was really pissed off that my mother called with such news, yet still kept on with her matter-of-fact style. Let me put it this way, I could envision her talking to me. She was a geriatric version of the old school TV sitcom mom character.

She had been a stay at home wife all of her life, in a neat little ranch house, on a nice little street in Skokie. She was certainly wearing a neat dress, some gaudy costume jewelry and taking her glasses off, then on, then off. She did it for effect during a conversation. I thought it was weird that she did it even while on the phone. I could just imagine her pulling off her glasses right after saying my Dad was in the hospital, or as she would call him, my father.

"He received an electrical shock, which caused him to fall. He ended up with a concussion. They just wanted him to stay overnight to be sure he was fine. He'll be home today."

"Electrocuted? What was he doing?"

"Well dear, your father asked me if I would like to go out for dinner Saturday night. We went to the restaurant inside the Marriot. Leigh, I don't know what got into us. We were just not ourselves." She actually gasped, but it was like she was excited and maybe bragging a little.

"What do you mean, Mom?"

"Well, it was very romantic. Before you know it, I kicked my shoes off and I was getting your father aroused with my feet!" ·

"Mom! My God, I do *not* want to know what freaky stuff you and daddy do!"

"Well, it isn't that bad. Your father did the most romantic thing ever. After we were done with our meal, he got a room for us."

"Why?" I think I was scowling like my cat at that point. "You guys live maybe fifteen minutes from there. Were you both drunk?"

"No, he just wanted to have a little change in atmosphere, I guess. I think he was actually role playing."

"What? Role playing? What the hell was he doing? Are you sure he didn't have a stroke or something?"

"Oh no, we went up to the room and he was just wild. Like an animal and it's so very unlike him, dear. When we had sex, he howled and said he was going to *shift*, I suppose that was very odd, but I assumed he meant to say he was going to cum."

"Oh my God, Mom! Please stop! How can you even tell me these things?" My mind was spinning and my brain needed to be bleached. This entire story sounded vaguely familiar, then it became crystal clear. This was just how my fictional characters had behaved in the scene I was writing.

"Well, he went to get up from the bed and he knocked over the lamp. He reached to grab it and put his finger right in the broken light socket. He just fell over and flopped around a little."

"But, he's OK though, right?"

"Yes, he's fine. As a matter of fact, he was making calls from the hospital this morning. He called the contractors that put the new roof on the garage last month. I guess he wants to let them know how much he appreciated their hard work, because he invited them over for a cookout in two weeks. You should really come down and visit for that weekend, Leigh. Those young men are about your age and I don't mind telling you that they are in great shape and very attractive."

"Mom!" Suddenly, I started to see that there was something strange going on. Not the fact that my Dad decided to throw together a cookout for some roofers, no, this was way too close to what I had written.

"Mom, let me call you back on that. Are you sure that inviting those guys to a cookout is a good idea? I mean, they are basically strangers."

I was getting worried. I hung up and grabbed my laptop from the desk. I looked over what I had completed on my story so far. Harry had taken his one true love Beatrice out for an elegant dinner that included nothing less than a foot job. "Holy shit!" I yelled to my cat. My horny characters got a luxury room that included, of course, a hot sex scene. Can you see the coincidence here? What did Harry say when he released his hot seed with a violent thrust from his rock hard shaft into the moist folds of his beloved? He howled and shouted, "I'm shifting." Which just happened to be at the height of his climax, before he shifted into a werewolf. "Oh shit!" I was a little relieved when I realized I didn't write anything about Harry getting electrocuted. Then, I saw the sentence. *Harry could feel the spark between them and it electrified his passion.* "Awe shit."

I had a problem. A big problem. Three werewolf hunters were about to break down the door to the room, chain Harry to a chair with silver, and force him to watch in horror as they completely dominated Beatrice in every forceful way you can imagine. The thing is, the evil Beatrice enjoyed tormenting her poor werewolf.

Somehow, I had magically made my parents literally reenact the steamy scene from my story, sans werewolf, a complete cuckhold gangbang was about to occur. "Oh my God!" I saw the wild and shameless scene of debauchery flash in my head. I cringed at the thought of my father getting tied up and gagged while watching my mother as she enjoyed being double penetrated by three porn star roofers. After I was done throwing up, I knew this was exactly what would happen at my parents little garden party in two weeks, and I had to prevent it. This was all my fault. But how? That is exactly what I am still trying to figure out.

Chapter Three

What Are Friends For?

Of course, at first, I suspected that someone had gotten to my story. I imagined ninjas dressed in black creeping through my windows. Then I realized that today's ninjas were hackers. Scratch the stealthy ninjas and bring on the creepy guy living in his parent's basement. There were probably empty soda cans and depleted bags of pork rinds scattered on the floor like peanut shells at a suburban cowboy steakhouse. That whole theory was impossible, since my laptop hasn't connected to the internet in months. Most likely it had to be the cat, but rather than confront her, I decided I would call on an expert.

My best friend, and marginally qualified high school English teacher, Kelly, might be able to help me to figure this out. Thankfully, she didn't possess half the fear of my psychotic cat that I did. When I say I'm afraid of my cat, it's because I have a good reason to be. I often wake up during the night to her growling at me. Some cats purr, some cuddle and knead, mine growls and hisses.

Kelly came by the apartment and I was relieved to have someone to talk to about what had happened. After I retold the entire story of my naughty writing and subsequent conversation with my mom, I eagerly awaited her advice.

"OK, Leigh, so let me get this straight. You think that everything you wrote, somehow wrote the future for what happened to your parents?"

"I think so, yeah. I don't know how it happened. I think my cat had something to do with it."

"Your cat. Your *cat*?" She said as her eyebrows arched. "You do realize how ridiculous that sounds, don't you?"

"You don't understand, Kelly. Luna is possessed. Once, when I was out of her treats, I came home without stopping at the store. She knew. She knew I didn't feel like stopping just for cat treats. She sat there and growled at me all evening. When I tried to pet her that night, she bit me! She actually drew blood! I still have the scar to prove it! I actually locked my bedroom door that night. And she is always acting very weird, spooky weird."

"Well, for now, let's concentrate on why this happened to your parents and not to some total strangers. Isn't your Dad's name Harold?"

"Ah! Why didn't I think of that! Yes, my Dad's name *is* Harold and Harry was the name of my character. The female character is Beatrice. My mom's name is Elizabeth though, so- oh shit! She has always gone by Elizabeth, but that is her middle name. Her first name *is* Beatrice. Oh my God, I need a shrink. Ugh! I wrote a paranormal erotica scene starring my parents. I bet a therapist could make a career out of that little issue."

"OK. Take it easy, Leigh. Let's assume that you stumbled on some magic. So why not put it to the test?"

"The test? What are you talking about and how exactly do I put it to the test?" I was bitchy and irritated. I should have realized my parents' names on my own, but Christ! To me my parents will always be Mom and Dad, not Beatrice and Harry, even if that's who they really are!

"Before you tinker around with your story any more, try a different story or idea. Do the same process as before, but a different story with different people. Make sure it's someone we know and you have to follow the steps exactly the same as you did before."

"That's a great idea. Who do you have in mind?"

"Hmm, well who do you know that is really deserving of having a fantasy fulfilled?"

I was quick to answer Kelly, considering that the two of us were perpetually single. "Me and you! But do you really want to take a leap like that? Experimenting on ourselves? What guys would we choose? What if we end up with complete losers? I know I'm not ready to set up some weird fantasy on myself. What if things go really, really bad? Nope. Not me. I don't think either of us are ready for something like that until we have a handle on this. Whatever *this* is."

"I've got it, Leigh! OK, so your sister is married. Why don't you write up a little romantic evening for the two of them? No paranormal, no BDSM, nothing kinky, just a good old fashioned love scene that ends up with incredible all night sex. What do you say? I bet it would do them some good."

"Sounds safe, but how will we know if it worked out like I wrote it?"

"Trust me, Leigh, no woman is going to have a night like that and not brag about it. You won't be able to shut her up! I guarantee, you will get a call the next morning."

"Ha! This could be fun. Still, I don't know if it will even work. If it *does* work, then it means that this whole thing isn't some strange coincidence and I will have to figure out *why* it is happening."

"Well, you have two weeks to figure it out. I have to run, but I'll check on you tomorrow. If this works… *I*'m next on the list. I haven't gotten laid in so long that I've been considering ordering one of those male mannequins with the interchangeable parts."

"What the hell are you talking about?"

"Yeah, they have these foam or plastic mannequins you can order now. They come with interchangeable parts, you know what I mean? You can literally pick your size and hook'em up. Ride'em cowgirl! They even come equipped with a rubber tongue." Kelly attempted to flick her tongue with an obscene lapping motion that made me wince when I pictured her awkwardly trying to squat over a plastic head with a rubber tongue flailing about.

"Jesus Christ, Kelly, now you've gone too far! Although, if you decide to try the rubber tongue man, you should record it for the next episode of America's Desperate Videos. You could become an internet sensation. Although, you might lose your job teaching." I would have to file this information away for use at a later date. I might need to get one of those mannequins for myself, now that my fantasies of my dear Vlad was crushed to bits. Need I even mention, how long it's been since I've had sex? I wondered if my hymen could have grown back. Yeah, it's been that long! "Do they really have ones with animatronic mouth parts?"

"Who knows? You know, I have my cousin Tim's wedding reception that I've been invited to. It promises to be a complete bore. Although, one of the groomsman is a doctor and I've always had a dirty little doctor-patient fantasy."

Kelly's encouraging words set aside any doubts I had. I set out to create a lovely, yet romantic evening for my dear unsuspecting sister, Sarah, and her utterly boring, and predictable husband, Bill. I wrote a nice romantic dinner date that followed up with a throbbing, earth shattering, and passion filled night for them. My sister had been married for eight years and already they had three kids that seemed to be sucking the joy and energy from her, like squalid feral baby vampires.

Whatever masculinity Bill had started with on their wedding day, had been relinquished at the altar. A career in banking scraped away any remnant of youth and sealed his fate. Sarah's days were consumed with juggling the myriad needs of two toddlers and a baby. I know she loves them, but I wonder if she ever sees her children carelessly drooling, vomiting, and defecating on the residue of her hopes and dreams. My poor sister and her husband seemed like they were willing unpaid participants in a chronic fatigue experiment gone horribly wrong. If anyone deserved a night of steamy, no-holds-barred passion, it was her and Bill.

I kept it fun and exciting, trying desperately to think of them solely as fictitious characters. I wanted Bill and Sarah to truly feel the things you can only read about, the normal things that is. It seemed a little weird at first using their names. I had to separate myself from the idea that this was my sister and her husband I was writing about. The only way to do that was for me to imagine completely different people that just so happened to share the names of Sarah and Bill.

Romance and Dinner

The dinner was fantastic, but it was nothing compared to the dessert that Sarah had planned for Bill. She had already prepared their bedroom in anticipation of the night's adventures. Sarah excused herself from the cozy candlelit dining room and then reappeared on the staircase wearing a sexy black negligée that left little to Bill's imagination. She aroused him by exposing one leg and running her fingers slowly up the inside of her thigh. She silently motioned for him to approach by beckoning him with her come-hither finger. He was throbbing with excitement and eagerly padded up the stairs after her. He passionately kissed her like he had never done before. Their tongues danced in each other's mouths and Bill impulsively picked her up and carried her to the bed. His rock hard passion wand was burning hot, but he wanted her to enjoy the experience of his tongue sliding across her soft folds and exploring her moist core. He wanted her to finally feel what it would be like to be awash in multiple orgasms while she firmly grasped his hair and pushed his face down to where she wanted him.

That was all I managed to type. How could I write a spectacular love scene when I, the writer, couldn't even stay awake long enough to do it? But it had been a long day for me and I dozed off before I could add any more to it. At three in the morning, I was woken up from my slouched over position on my desk by Luna's needle sharp claws piercing the skin on my leg.

"God damn cat!" I yelled at her. When she did things like this, I often contemplated returning her to the shelter where I adopted her. Sadly, no matter how much I bitched about Luna, I still loved the little freak. There were those few blissful moments where she was actually affectionate and that seemed to make it all worth it- most of the time!

She just stared at me and then walked away into the shadows. I stumbled off to my bed and drifted back into a deep, restful sleep.

Chapter Four

Earthquakes and ER visits

The morning came without incident. That is no phone calls, no messages, nothing from my sister. I plodded around the kitchen and shook off the cobwebs. I heated up the tea kettle for a cup of tea and I filled a bowl with my favorite cereal and milk. This was the one time of day that Luna was sweet to me. She jumped up on the counter and brought her whiskers close to the bowl. I took a small bowl of milk and I let Luna lap it up while I ate.

I watched her as I tore the roof of my mouth open on Captain Crunch. I thought about how cats are such strange pets. With having the complete knowledge that you are about to invite a paranoid schizophrenic creature into your home… to live with you, would you still do it? A cat owner does. How about willingly adopting a creature that the English language can't even describe in a single word. You know, someone who experiences a dark satisfying pleasure through maliciously ruining someone's life and then rejoicing as they witness the other person's misfortune? The Germans have a word for that evil person, schadenfreude. I have a word too, cat. You can enter the phrase domestic medium-hair into the description.

I thought about calling Sarah, the suspense was killing me. Did my experiment have any affect? I realized I hadn't written that much, but from previous conversations with Sarah, I had learned one of the greatest disappointments of her marriage was that Bill was not orally inclined. She remarked that he seemed timid and reluctant to participate in enjoying what she called a "taco dinner." I cringed every damn time she called it a "taco dinner." Who the hell refers to getting what could be the absolute in oral pleasure as a fucking "taco dinner?"

I knew that from what I wrote, she should have at least been ecstatic in the change that came over Bill. I held off and spent my morning lounging around in the laziest Sunday morning mode possible. By noon, I couldn't take it any longer, I called Sarah.

"Hey, Sarah! So how's your weekend so far?" I crossed my fingers and winced, waiting for some great news about Sarah's glorious passionate night.

"Oh, just the same old thing. We finally corralled the little monsters into bed and for once we planned to watch a movie, but we both fell asleep."

"Really? That's all? I mean, I'm sorry. I guess being Mom to those little cuties can really take the steam out of a girl."

Our conversation digressed into a number of trivial topics before we said goodbye. Once I had ended the call, I sat down and wondered if in fact, I had drawn too much of a conclusion from my parents incident. I've done it before. Something similar had happened when I was in grade school. Let's just admit it. Every little girl daydreams at some point about having magic powers. I know I did.

All kids operate within the doctrine of a primitive belief system, where there is no such thing as a coincidence. A kid gets the hiccups simply because they were sassing their mom, or it was raining because they were sad. Well, I would imagine myself as a long lost descendent of a Salem witch. Of course, it didn't matter that I was a descendant of Jewish grandparents that emigrated from Belgium in the 1920's. Kids can overlook tiny details like that with a little use of their imaginations. So it was with me.

Nathan Burnside was his name and he was a habitual thorn in my side. I could never forget that kid. He picked on me relentlessly for no reason. It was what he liked to do for shits and giggles. I imagined that I was able to use my awesome super powers for revenge against his scruffy little ass. Looking back, I'm sure there must have been a million kids like me. We all fantasized about being able to take down our bully with a simple wiggle of our finger. Then it happened. Nathan was out in front of the school, with his little trolls, pushing, shoving, and berating some poor little boy. From behind a large tree trunk, I wiggled my finger and wished a curse on him. I no sooner completed my magic spell, when a large branch blew down from the tree above him. It caught everyone by surprise, including me.

The limb came down and nailed Nathan with a direct hit. I confidently marched over to his fallen body while he writhed in pain. It must have been quite a sight, a nine year old girl waiving her finger at her vanquished bully. I shouted at him, "I've got powers! And I'm not afraid to use them!"

I'm sure I would have been a fresh target for every bully and troll present, but it was hard to argue with the fact that Nathan had his collar bone broken by my mere finger wag. In time, I realized the old tree branch was an accident waiting to happen and it was quite convenient for it to have hit a target like that little asshole.

Now, back to the problem at hand. I supposed, I could have possibly been making my parents electrifying sexual encounter out as something much more than it was. Perhaps, it was just the shock of having my mother actually tell me the intimate details. I was so completely distraught that I *thought* I heard her say things that matched my story. In other words, I was reading way too much into my own writing. There. Done. I was satisfied that no problem really existed and it was back to taking out my sexual and emotional frustrations on writing a wonderfully raunchy story. I finally felt absolutely liberated to write freely, even if I never intended to publish a word of it. I found that writing was a good form of therapy for my twisted and warped mind.

That afternoon, I began to write once again. I imagined a new story line that would include plenty of hot and heavy sex, because I damn sure needed it. I always imagined a "surprise" scene, the kind where the woman meets a super-hot, yet complete stranger. The kind of stranger with thick, dark, yet cropped hair, smoldering eyes, and let's not forget the beautiful six pack abs we all fantasize about lazily running our tongues over. The stranger takes complete control and gives the woman everything she could ever want from a lover and more, without her ever having to ask for it. It's like he knows her inner most thoughts and sexual desires and fulfills them perfectly. Of course, she is more than willing to engage in a little harmless BDSM to achieve her wildest thoughts. I mean, really, who wouldn't want that? Rock my world... please!

I should state, just for the record, and even though it sounds fun as hell. It's not something I would ever do in real life, not in a million years. Yet the thought of the storyline had my mind reeling with excitement. In a world of fantasy, what's wrong with a little fun and a harmless slutty encounter? Just in case, I avoided

using the names of any real people that
I knew.

Clean-up in aisle three

George didn't mind stocking the
grocery store shelves at night. The
heavier the boxes were, the better of a
workout he got. After all, he needed to
stay in top shape, as his male modeling
career was just about to take off. Few
people came in at the late hour and he
enjoyed the peace and quiet.

Brandy was a take charge girl. Her
days were filled with kicking corporate
ass and taking boardroom names. She
didn't have time for relationships, but
she had her needs. Needs that could
easily be taken care of by that stock
boy lifting those boxes up over his
head. She watched him intently, letting
her desire build up. She was a wild
cat, a huntress, preparing to take down
her prey and devour him. She was still
in her business attire and she let her
hair loose from its updo. Her black
hair cascaded down over her back in
preparation for her move.

The timing was right. He had
stopped to lift his t-shirt up and wipe
his forehead. He revealed a rock hard
set of sculpted abs and pecs to the

woman at the end of the aisle and he knew it. George wasn't shy and he often delighted in the way women came into the store and drooled over him. It stoked his already over confident ego.

Brandy walked up to him and grabbed his ass with one hand and let her other hand run down his chest. She looked at him as though she were going to eat him alive. When she spoke, her throaty voice came out as more of a growl than the purr she intended. "I don't want to know your name, I don't want your number. I just want this." She grabbed the bulge that was easily visible through his jeans. "Now, get into that back office and fuck me."

"Yes, ma'am." George knew this type of woman, and he had no problem with her direct approach. They walked into the small office that was situated behind the vegetable section. She pushed him back and down onto the desk and immediately unzipped his jeans. She appreciated that his erection was hard, ready, and huge. She pulled his jeans off of him and then she wasted no time in tossing off her jacket and her skirt. She climbed on top of him and rode him until she was overcome with an earth shattering orgasm.

I didn't think it was too bad, after all, I was just getting started at this. Mostly, it was fun to write. I had no immediate intention of actually using this or any other story for anything more than my own amusement. I added it to the file of steamy snippets along with Sarah and Bill's mouthwatering romp.

When I woke up the next day, I was quite relieved at not having to worry about some freaky paranormal activity occurring in my life. It was a huge weight taken off of my shoulders. I relaxed and turned on the local news. During the night a natural gas line had apparently ruptured under the city streets. It centered on the block that housed the local grocery store. The force of the explosion was so violent that it cracked the sidewalks, split the asphalt on the street, and shattered the windows from the grocery store. The station was running news feeds of the witnesses that were caught in the disaster. My attention was diverted by my phone ringing. It was Kelly.

"Leigh! Did you see the news?"

"A little, something about a gas line explosion down at the Safeway. I sure hope nobody got hurt."

"No, I guess everyone is OK. Watch the news. My cousin was in the store when it happened! They interviewed her and some of the others. You watching?"

"Yeah, I am. It looks like they are just now starting to run the on-site interviews."

"There! There she is! That's my cousin, Brandy!"

"Brandy?" I sat down on the arm of the couch. I knew this was bad news.

A disheveled and bewildered woman of about thirty appeared on the screen. She had a Safeway shirt wrapped around her waist and her blouse was unbuttoned.

"Why is your cousin half naked at a grocery store?" I was hoping maybe she was afflicted with some unusual psychological condition that caused her to impulsively strip while picking up some ice cream.

"Just watch, they ran this earlier. You are not going to believe it."

Brandy was seemingly in shock and didn't respond to the reporter's nagging questions. A young, well-built man was walking in the background. More like slinking away. He was naked and was keeping his waist covered with a piece of cardboard.

Kelly was rejoicing in the scene. "Ha ha! I always knew Brandy was a slut. She was fucking that guy when that explosion happened. I just know it. So obvious! I wonder what she'll have to say-"

I interrupted Kelly as she gloated over her cousin's embarrassment. "Kelly, I wrote that. Not the explosion exactly, but I wrote a scene about a woman named Brandy who screws a Safeway worker."

"Huh? Why in the hell would you write that? I didn't even know you knew Brandy."

"No! No, I don't know her. I was just playing around with some writing, and I tried to use names of people that I didn't know. Damn it!"

"Don't feel too bad, Leigh. If you wouldn't have wrote it, she would have been screwing some other stranger. What about the explosion? Why did you blow up the Safeway? I sure hope it wasn't because they stopped selling your favorite chip dip."

"Of course not. But that isn't a bad idea. I freakin' loved the old dip. Bastards." I had to run to my desk and open the story. That was it. I HAD blown up the store. Then I read the words out loud to Kelly. "She was overcome with an earth shattering orgasm. That's what I wrote."

Kelly gasped audibly through my phone. "Fuck- no wonder she couldn't talk. Earth shattering? Really, Leigh?" Then she asked me apprehensively, "Leigh, what other stuff did you write?"

"Nothing. Well, I wrote something about Sarah and Bill the night before, but apparently nothing happened to them. I asked my sister how her night was and she said they fell asleep watching a movie."

"Well, you better check back with them today. Maybe there is a delayed reaction or something to this magic."

I wandered around my living room, trying to absorb what had happened. I needed to come to grips with the magic once again. "Damn it!" I yelled and then I called Sarah. There was no answer, so I left a message for her to call me back as soon as possible. I waited a couple of hours before I tried again. After I left another message, I truly worried. Sarah was always home on Mondays. It was early afternoon when I finally got a call back from her.

"How's it going, Sarah? I was getting worried, usually I hear back from you pretty quickly."

"Oh, well, I had a little medical issue. Everything is fine now, no worries."

"Medical issue? You can't just say that you had some medical issue and not tell your only sister!"

"Fine, I have to warn you though, it's pretty embarrassing." She sounded shaky and unsure. There was no way in hell that she was *NOT* going to tell me what happened. I would drive to her house right this second if I had to, though it would be a pretty long drive as I lived in Illinois and she lived in Pennsylvania.

"Spill it!" I demanded.

"The other day, I decided that Bill and I were way overdue for a nice romantic evening. We really were. I had hoped to set it up for Saturday night, but the kids where little psychos all day and we were completely worn out. So I arranged it for last night. Nothing crazy, just a nice dinner and then, you know, a little grown-up time in the bedroom."

"Sounds nice!" I tried to sound cheerful, but I was biting my lower lip. I knew she was about to drop the other shoe.

"It started out great. Awesome in fact. I have to tell you that everything I told you about Bill lacking in oral skills can be dismissed. He was like a professional or something. I've never experienced an orgasm by anyone eating my taco before- well, at least not with Bill. It was incredible, Leigh. Multiple times. Over and over."

"Woohoo! Congratulations! Happy to hear it!"

"The thing is, even when he stopped, I didn't. I was stuck in a full-blown orgasm. We tried everything to get it to stop. He thought maybe I needed more, you know, from him. Let me tell you, he was frickin' engorged, too. It didn't matter because I was still stuck on O. And he couldn't do much of anything because he said his thing was burning."

"His thing? Burning?"

"Yeah, you know, his penis. He had an erection that wouldn't go away. He couldn't do anything with it because he said it felt like it was burning inside. While my orgasm was fun at first it became painful, then it went beyond painful, it was killing me. I've had three kids and this was like the worst contraction, only it didn't come and go, it just stayed."

"Oh my God!"

"Yeah, well this went on for almost four hours. I accused him of getting Viagra and spiking my drink with it or something else. We were both in so much pain that neither of us could drive to the emergency room, but we both knew that we needed help. Bill called for an ambulance. Then he called over to the neighbors and asked if they could stay with the kids for a little while. It was so embarrassing. I can't even begin to explain just how awful it was to have two paramedics here chuckling over my predicament. They couldn't even touch me. When the guy pulled back the sheet to examine me, or to see if there was anything wrong, he touched me down there. I started screaming. According to Bill, I was completely out of my mind. Apparently, I told them that they should all fuck me and get it over with. He said, I was begging for double penetration. Of course they didn't. I'm sure that I will be the laughing stock of the entire hospital. I hope, I never have any other ailments that send me to the emergency room, because they will likely never forget me or Bill. Not to mention the fact, I would be too embarrassed to show my face there, ever again. At this point, Leigh, I would rather die of a heart attack than seek medical attention at the ER. It's probably on the internet by now, but I'm too afraid to go look."

"Oh God, Sarah, I am so sorry. I didn't- I mean, I would never want to experience something so awful. So what did they do? How did they fix your, uh, problems?"

"We got an ambulance ride. Yep. Bill and his fiery cock and me with my painful pussy. What a pair we were coming into the ER! Every doctor and every nurse came in to check us out. Poor Bill was diagnosed with priapism. They took a needle and drained blood from the vessels in his engorged penis. I was sedated with something through an IV. I have no idea, I can't remember a thing after that. We were both discharged late into the night and had to take a cab home. Ugh, Leigh. It was the worst experience. I am afraid we won't be having any sort of sex for a long time."

"You're OK now, though. Right? No residual effects?"

"Yes, we are both OK, just scared to death to start anything sexual now."

After the phone call, I was floored. Back to the drawing board, once again. Now, how could I have caused *that* mess? I scrolled through the half-finished story. Then I saw it. Fuck, Fuck, Fuck! Did I really write that? *His rock hard passion wand was burning hot.* That explained Bill's little problem. Half finished! I left it half finished! That's what happened to Sarah and why she ended up in the ER with an unstoppable orgasm. I had written to the point where she was experiencing an uncontrollable orgasm and I fell asleep for hours. It was no coincidence. Sarah's ER visit was directly related to me leaving her fictional self in a state of bliss. I didn't know whether I should laugh or cry. The thought of my sister ending up at the emergency room because of me writing a sex scene for her was not good, but her begging for all of the EMT's to fuck her and becoming a regular joke at the ER- PRICELESS!

Chapter 5

White Magic, Safety First!

Time was running out. I knew for certain that I was able to affect the love lives of just about anyone with my new found power. I guess you could say, I had become the witch I once daydreamed about, although, I didn't know how it happened. In a way, it made me feel invincible. If I wanted to let my dark side out, I could really fuck up someone's day. I'm just not that kind of girl. Really, I do try to have a sense of morals. Any good woman will tell you, I may be an angel, but fuck with me and the halo is coming off. You can bet your ass the horns are coming out!

I needed another test. I needed to see if I would have the same effect on something completely nonromantic. If I could succeed at that, then I would be able to easily make adjustments to my parents' upcoming dinner party. I had to think of something that really couldn't go wrong. In adherence to the code of all good witches, I wouldn't use it for my own benefit.

I started thinking about the people I knew that could use a little boost in their lives. There was Lindsey, I remember she had complained about needing her roof worked on. My friend, Jennifer hadn't taken a day off of her job in 30 years. She needed a vacation. Then there was Kim, who had been driving the same piece of junk car since she got her driver's license. I figured, if I very carefully wrote something for each of them, I could do something really good for all of them. I would just have to write it as a snippet within a story.

It was time to whip up some white magic. Without a clue as to how any of my magic worked, I sat down at my little antique writing desk and started with my first victim. Poor choice for words, I know. Don't worry, I'll explain.

A new roof for Lindsey

Lindsey looked up and saw yet another tiny but steady cascade of water dripping down from the ceiling in her kitchen. She selected an empty coffee can and set it in place to catch the droplets of water. If this kept happening, she would be out of cans, pans, tubs, and pails. It was a disaster. The problem was the roof on her old house had simply exceeded the life expectancy of the old shingles.

Not only were they no longer functional, they made the house look like hell.

Lindsey was one to always sign up for the promotional giveaways in the stores she went to. It didn't matter that she never actually won, it was the hope of winning that pushed her along. Today was different. Her phone rang, and when she answered the call, she nearly fainted. The man calling her said she had won the home improvement grand prize from Big Box Home and Garden. The value of the prize was limited to a home improvement project that didn't exceed $8,000. She was ecstatic. Finally, her efforts of frantically scribbling her personal information down and stuffing it into the overflowing cardboard displays had paid off. They would be sending an estimator to her home that afternoon. How much better could her day have gone?

Next up was Jennifer and a long overdue vacation.

Cruising with Jennifer

It was more like a parking lot out on the interstate during rush hour, but day after day she dutifully climbed into her car and prepared herself for another ninety minutes of sweltering *torture, otherwise known as The Commute. Normally, road rage set in for Jennifer at about twenty minutes into the drive. Today, traffic was at a standstill. Her doctor told her during her fifty year physical that she needed to find ways to relax. It just wasn't healthy to get so stressed out over the traffic. The doctor said the stress would take years off of her life. Jennifer thought of it as a positive for her. She figured about another month of this and she would be all the way back to twenty years old again.*

Jennifer bounced from radio station to radio station until she found something relaxing. Before long, the DJ began to announce the daily trivia contest winners. Jennifer cranked up the volume and intently listened. She had been hoping for months that she would be the lucky one to be selected for the grand prize. It would be heaven, a seven day all inclusive Caribbean cruise. The DJ rambled on and on. "Jesus! Would you just tell us who won already?" Jennifer occasionally pressed down on her horn and shouted obscene epithets for poor drivers while she waited for the announcement. Then it came, a grand prize winner had been selected. The catch was that they had to take an immediate cruise, leaving from Houston in just two days. The winner would be announced after the commercial break. "Oh, easy! That's a piece of cake for me. I'm already in Houston and I am just dying to get out of this boxed-in traffic, and boxed-in life." Traffic finally broke free and she shouted out to the broken down pickup truck that had been holding everyone up. "Hey, you! With that piece of junk, why don't ya tie a quarter to it and throw it away, and you can say you lost something! And take yer ugly girlfriend with ya!"

The woman in the truck shouted back at Jennifer, "Who you calling ugly?"

Jennifer was a Texan, and by God, she loved every chance she had at using her full repertoire of Southern euphemisms. "You! You're so ugly, you probably have to slap your feet to get them to go to bed with you! You're so ugly, you look like you were pulled through a knothole backwards! You're so ugly-"

"Yeah, yeah, we get it! She's ugly! Let's move!" The people in the car behind her shouted.

Jennifer was still listening to the radio as she made her way forward through the snarled traffic. When the DJ came back on the air, he finally made his announcement. Jennifer screamed with joy as she heard her name called. Finally, Jennifer was going to get out of the box and experience a true awakening! Further down the road she said to herself, "Well, no lie. That woman was ugly. She looked like she sorts bobcats for a livin'."

Not to be forgotten was my third friend, Kim. She not only needed a new car, she deserved one. She worked like mad and got nowhere fast. I really wanted to help her out in any way that I could!

It's a Brand New Car!

Kim was ecstatic. She had been waiting for weeks for this day. She had been selected as a contestant on the top listed TV game show Fortune Wheel. They were coming to Chicago this week and Kim was primed. She had been doing crossword puzzles in every spare minute and more. She even woke up an hour early every day to squeeze in more prep time, before the big show.

When Kim was finally called to the podium, she felt nervous yet confident that she was well prepared to solve every word puzzle that Janna could throw at her. It was ridiculously easy.

Every spin of the wheel landed her more cash. She solved every puzzle, leaving her fellow competitors standing there open-mouthed with shock and awe.

The time had come for the final puzzle and the grand prize. A new car! It was a beauty. Her dream car. A yellow Mustang with black racing stripes and it was fully loaded with every possible option. Fortune smiled on Kim that day.

Now, how could anything bad happen? With wonderful, happy stories like these, I was certain that I would have three very happy friends. My phone rang and I cheerfully answered. It was Kelly, she wanted to know if anything happened with Sarah and Bill. I told her everything that happened with the hot date night that ended up at the ER. Kelly was in full agreement with my new plan to test out some white magic. All I had to do now, was to wait for the good news to come rolling in.

I remembered to ask Kelly about the wedding she attended. I wanted the scoop on the doctor. Inquiring minds needed to know if he was panty wetting hot, drop dead gorgeous, or just finger licking good. "What about that doctor you were hoping to hook up with!"

"Oh, he got called in to the hospital, I guess. The wedding was nice, but as far as meeting anyone, it was a complete failure."

I started to hatch a plan. "Oh, that's too bad. What was the doctor's name?"

"Florian. Florian Klempner. I know, the name sounds horrid. I can't even imagine what somebody with a name like that would be like, but he is a young single doctor and those don't come around very often, if at all."

"That's true. Too bad, huh? Well, sorry to hear that."

"That's OK. I have to run though. I'm supposed to drop off the shoes I borrowed for the wedding. She needs them back today."

I knew I had to write one more little story. Very short and sweet. Just to put a spark under Florian's ass. After we hung up, I went back to my desk.

Phone call for Kelly!

Kelly was wondering how the wedding could have went had she gotten a chance to meet up with the doctor that couldn't make it. She thought, perhaps there would be another chance

55

someday. She really didn't know anything about him. What kind of doctor was he? Was he good looking? Kelly tried to relax and slouched in her favorite comfortable chair and tried not to think about it. She had just opened up a hot new romance book and began to read when her phone rang.

"Hello?"

"Hi, Kelly? This is Florian, Florian Klempner."

"Oh! Hi. You're the guy that was supposed to be my date for the wedding! How are you?"

"I'm fine, thanks. I got your number from your cousin. Sorry, but when I'm on the on-call rotation schedule, things get really crazy for me. I hope you don't mind that I asked your cousin for your number. I just wanted to apologize for skipping out on you."

"Oh, don't worry about it. It's perfectly understandable. Everyone knows what a huge responsibility it is to be a doctor and all."

"Well, I have a question for you. How would you feel about going out on a date? I understand that it's unexpected and basically a blind date."

"I'd love to! What do you have in mind?"

"I was wondering if you were free this evening, we could go out to eat. There's a new Thai place that I've been wanting to check out. I've heard great things about it. How does that sound?"

"Sounds great, Florian. The only thing is that we need to drop by my sister's house for a minute. I promised I would drop off some shoes I borrowed."

"How about five o'clock, then? I just need your address. Oh and my friends call me Bob. Yeah, Florian isn't the name I would have picked."

"Ha ha, no problem, Bob. It's 2771 Monroe. It's a tiny little white house with blue shutters. I'm looking forward to meeting you.

"Sounds great, Kelly. See you at five then."

I wanted to pat myself on the back. I managed to come up with four great stories for my friends. Lindsey would get a new roof, Jennifer would get the vacation she deserved, Kim would get a shiny new set of wheels, and now Kelly would finally meet up with the doctor.

Chapter Six

Leigh - Paranormal Investigator

Now that I had a few experiments set up, I had some time to try to figure out why all of this crazy stuff was happening. I knew the only thing that had changed in my house was the procurement of the antique desk. I took a close look at it. It was pretty plain. The small drawer at the front was empty when I brought it home. I pulled it out and looked into the recess where the drawer had been. Nothing. I set the drawer down and crouched under the desk to see if I could spot anything out of the ordinary. Again, I found nothing.

I became distracted by Luna who was pleading for her food. I went to the kitchen and filled her dish with her favorite fatty catty food, but when I called her, she wouldn't come. She continued to cry from the other room. I went to find out what her problem was. She was laying down with her front paws extended over the drawer. There, between her paws, I could make out a small section that was covered in faded writing on the bottom of the drawer. The writing wasn't in English. I shooed the cat away and brought the drawer up to my desk lamp to get a closer look. The strange writing appeared to be Latin.

Cave quid dicis, quando, et cui

I don't know any Latin. This was a job for my internet research partner, Google, more specifically. Thank God, my internet had been restored and I could finally connect to the world again. I sat down at my computer and entered the words into the search bar. The translation shocked me with how appropriate it was for my situation.

Beware of what you say, when, and to whom.

Exactly. You got that right. Who wrote this? Where on earth did this desk come from? I scrambled through the papers that I had removed from the drawer. I'll admit it, I'm a pack rat. I never throw away any sort of correspondence, notes, lists, or receipts. Somewhere in the mess, I had to have kept the piece of paper with the phone number and address of the place where I picked up the desk. I had more than a few serious questions for the old lady. I rustled through the papers until I found it. I quickly dialed the phone number and fortunately someone answered.

"Hello." It was the same grumpy old woman I talked to months ago.

"Hi, my name is Leigh. I'm the one who picked up your old desk-"

The call hung up. "Bitch!" I yelled. "Rude!" I hate getting hung up on, even when it's a wrong number. Which could have been the case. I carefully dialed it again rather than opting for the redial feature.

"Hello." Said the same crusty voice.

"Please, don't hang up on me. Please?" I thought if I pleaded in a helpless voice, she would have some mercy and talk to me.

"What is it?" Although she said it more like a statement than a question.

"All I want to know is a little history on the desk. You see, someone is very interested in buying it from me, and they would like to know some of its history. I would be willing to split the sale price with you, if you help me out." I lied through my teeth.

Bingo! Money talks. She started to tell me something. "It is very old. It came from someplace in New England. Massachusetts, I think."

"Thank you! How old do you think it is? Do you know who owned it before? Or perhaps you know the story of who wrote on the bottom of the drawer, in Latin?"

"Listen to me little girl, if someone is willing to buy that desk from you, sell it, give it away. Whatever you do with it, you must not destroy it or your problem will only get worse. That desk is a curse. It belonged to a witch. I think you have found out already that it casts spells. Magic has consequences and you must have found that out, as well, or you wouldn't have called me."

"Fine. I'm sorry for lying to you. Nobody wants to buy it. It's causing everything I write to happen to people I know. Literally! I know I can handle this. I just want to know one thing. Who was the witch?"

"That is all I know. Goodbye."

"Wait, I-"

That was it. The end of the call. The bitty old bitch hung up on me again! I did learn something, or at least I confirmed my suspicions. It was the desk, and I wasn't the first person to experience its so-called curse. The way I look at it, this desk was bewitched for a good reason, and it even came with its very own warning label!

I really wanted to know more about this original witch. Who was she? Where in New England? Could it have been Massachusetts? Could it be? Imagine if my very desk was used by a genuine Salem witch! Then again, I don't think they were writers. I think they were young girls and midwives. Back to my best friend, the internet. I needed to learn more about witches in Massachusetts. I wondered if any writers were ever accused of being witches. There were none that I found in my search, although there were a few very educated and prominent people accused of it. Perhaps, someone who had survived the nonsense of the Salem witch trials decided to actually seek revenge later by trying their hand at *real* witchcraft? Now, that would be a great form of payback. Maybe, just maybe, someone figured out a way to cast spells through writing out scenarios for their victims!

For now, I was satisfied I had enough information to consider that with the power vested in my desk, I was officially a witch. My heart jumped a little with glee. OK, once I admitted it to myself, I actually jumped for joy. Trust me, this was a childhood dream come true! Sure, I was apprehensive about it all. Once I had talked to the old woman and confirmed my suspicions, I decided to embrace it. This could be great! After all, look at all of the white magic spells I wrote already. Who says that I would need to be the stereotypical Halloween witch? Modern fiction was full of fun and sexy witches and I really was one of them now!

I was overjoyed when morning came, because I knew good reports would start rolling in from my friends. The first call came from Lindsey. She told me the wonderful news about winning the home improvement prize. What was probably even more magical, was that the roofers were already at her house and had started to work. Lindsey told me, there were three young men on the crew. She described them as a virtual buffet of delectable and mouthwatering man snacks. She must have been hungry. I had a great idea. It was a warm summer day, we were teachers on summer break and we deserved to have a picnic. I called Kelly and left her a message to come over to Lindsey's house at noon. I let her know that swimsuits and cold adult beverages were required.

Chapter Seven

A Hot Picnic

I showed up at Lindsey's house at noon. I brought the essentials, suntan oil, a couple of folding beach chairs, and the skimpiest two piece swimsuit I owned. I glanced up at the guys on the roof as I walked in through Lindsey's front door. She was right. Her house was crawling with hotties. How exciting! We met in the kitchen for a bit and laughed about her good fortune. I didn't say a thing about the little spell I had written. We headed into another room and changed into our skimpy little bikinis. Now, we aren't supermodels, but I think we looked damn hot, except for the fact that our pale skin made us look like we had spent our entire lives living in an underground mushroom farm.

We placed our chairs in the backyard, facing the house. With a cooler full of hard lemonade between us, we watched the show. The guys working on the roof had already stripped off their t-shirts and were covered in sweat. Their hot, toned bodies were well tanned and every bit as scrumptious as Lindsey had described. Kelly arrived and noticed how we had set up to ogle the roofers.

"Holy man feast! How do I get three hot men to pound on my roof?"

Lindsey and I laughed hysterically at the look on Kelly's face as she darted into the house to get changed. Once she came out of the door, she jogged over to where we set up her chair. Drinks in hand, we continued to watch the panty melting entertainment.

Kelly came up with a little game. "So, what do you say, how about we start by choosing which one has the best arms?"

That was easy, there was one guy whose arms were just incredible. Any girl will tell you that nothing tops off a muscular arm like having nicely developed deltoids, those rounded upper arm bulges… YUM!

"I have one!" Shouted Lindsey." Let's vote on which one has the best lines or vines or whatever they're called. The ones that run along his abs and then down and in, on the hips. Those are the best thing to look at, in my opinion. It's like they are just guiding your eyes down to the prize. Like a big Vegas style neon sign."

This took a considerable amount of time to study. They were all in such good shape, but because of the distance and the fact that they were moving around so much, it was difficult to tell. Lindsey surprised us when she called out to the roofers, "Hey, would you guys like to take a break and grab a bottle of water?" Kelly and I looked at her with both shock and amusement. She looked at us and said, "OK, now is our chance, get a close look and decide for yourselves."

One by one the guys came down the ladders and started to walk over to us. We had already been sipping on our hard lemonades for a while, so none of us were about to be quiet or shy. We were all giggling like school girls. This promised to be fun. Kelly opened a cooler and tossed them each a water bottle. The situation wasn't lost on the boys either. They could tell we had been checking them out, and they put on their best display of flirtation.

The alcohol must have really hit Lindsey, because she got right to the point.

"OK, we want you guys to all stand in a line facing us. We are trying to decide on something."

Thankfully, they were good sports and lined up a foot away from Lindsey. Kelly and I came closer and we started judging. We asked them questions that probably surprised them.

"So, do you guys work out?" "Do you have a girlfriend?" And of course Lindsey, "Would you LIKE a girlfriend?"

The scenario was swiftly digressing into a scene more likely to happen at a bachelorette party. Lindsey started to run her hand over their chests and stomachs and then said, "You guys don't mind, do you? We are just trying to judge who has the best… parts."

Of course, the guys loved the attention, and they started asking Kelly and I to come over and check it out. Kelly was getting a little too carried away on one guy that she apparently really liked. His jeans hung quite low and her hand kept sliding down to the waistband. It became obvious by the huge bulge rising up, he liked what she was doing.

I started to worry that someone would see us and wonder if we were going to start a backyard orgy. I had to break it up. "OK guys, turn around."

Kelly said very loudly, "Yeah, let's get a good look at your asses." And she wasted no time in patting the ass in front of her.

"OK guys, back to work. The roof isn't going to put itself on!" Lindsey surprised us and we booed her. "When you get done for the day, I can start the grill and make some dinner for you. Would that be OK?"

They were all in agreement and hustled back onto the roof to work with renewed vigor. It was a glorious day to be young and single. I had a shadow of doubt about Lindsey's proposition to them, though. I thought about how at this pace, we would be quite drunk by dinner time. With all of the flirting going on, there was no telling how this was going to end up.

I decided to drag the attention away from the workers for a few minutes, because the more I thought about it, the more naughty thoughts came to mind. I remembered my magic spell to get the doctor to call Kelly.

"Hey, Kelly, What were you up to last night? I looked for you online, but didn't see you."

"Oh- nothing special." She quietly hung her head.

I knew that look of embarrassment, so of course, I had to seize the moment. "OK, something happened. Spit it out!"

"OK, well you remember that doctor I was supposed to meet at the wedding, but he never showed? Well, he called me yesterday."

"And?" I asked, wondering why she would try to hide it. This was normally something that would make her shout to the heavens. I, however, was filled with a sudden rush of curiosity and anxiousness. This had to have gone right for her. My magic had to have worked!

"Well, what happened?" Lindsey was just as curious.

"He came by and picked me up to go out to a new Thai restaurant he wanted to check out. Let me tell you something, he is nothing at all like I imagined."

"What? You mean all young doctors don't look like the ones on TV?" I laughingly asked.

"No! Not even close. He is about five feet tall. Scrawny. So scrawny. He has the physique of a twelve year old boy with red hair that he mousses up to make himself look taller. He looked like one of those fucking troll dolls."

"Ha ha!" Lindsey and I were in tears with laughter.

"Oh, it gets worse, much worse. I never asked what kind of doctor he was. I assumed that since he got called in during the wedding that perhaps he was a skilled surgeon or an ER doctor. Well, we had to stop by my sister's house on our way to the restaurant so I could drop off the shoes I borrowed. My nephew asked him straight up what kind of doctor he was. Ugh!"

"Ugh? Come on, you are killing us. Just tell us!" I begged.

"He told my nephew that he is a urologist. So, you all know how curious my nephew is. He asked him what kind of doctor that was. Needless to say, my nephew took full advantage of that, like any seven year old would. He ran around the house announcing, 'Auntie Kelly's boyfriend is a pee-pee doctor!'

We were roaring with laughter. I had to console her. "Oh, come on. That isn't so bad. At least he is a doctor and a specialist!"

Lindsey chimed in, "Yeah, Kelly! A specialist! Maybe he knows some good pee-pee tricks."

We were laughing so hard that it was almost unbearable. Poor Kelly. She wasn't helping her cause.

"Sorry to say, I don't want to find out. I was seriously sick to my stomach, and I cancelled dinner plans right there on the spot. I was physically ill. I got this visual in my head of Florian the troll boy working over a geriatric man's shriveled twig. Or examining warts on another. I imagined horrid venereal diseases and prostate exams. God forbid, I ever let him touch me. I mean, it's not like guys with normal, healthy penises have to go get the Florian special. Just the sick ones. Yuck."

"Seriously." I could barely speak and my sides hurt, I was laughing so hard. "You're killing me! Stop!"

Lindsey was twice as hammered as we were. "Oh, let's call Florian up! I want to ask him some things! Imagine the bizarre stories he can tell us!"

"NO!" Kelly and I said in unison.

"I for one, would like to think of the penis as something- nice. It should be thought of as something to appreciate or something that is awesome to play with. I don't want to hear a bunch of sick stories and get disgusting images trapped in my head!"

"Well said, Leigh!" Kelly commented as she nodded to the roofers. "Now, those guys. What about them? I should have asked them to show us their penises."

"Such a slut!" I joked. "Actually, I don't like it being referred to as a penis. That seems too clinical, dick sounds too raunchy and pecker or wiener are just childish. And willie- well, that sounds like something only a sideshow freak would say! From now on, just call it a cock. I like the sound of that. Cock. As in a big, thick cock. Yep! And, Kelly, back to your request, don't you think that would be going a little overboard? Have some shame!"

"Shame? Huh? Well, it's not every day you are overrun with hunks. There shall be no shame in this house today!" She lifted her drink up, as if she were toasting to her good fortune.

The rest of the afternoon was spent watching the guys on the roof and getting quite drunk. I realized, it was a good thing I wasn't in close proximity to my magic desk or we would have quite the situation on our hands. I looked at my phone and noticed it was nearly four o'clock. Nobody was going to be driving anywhere tonight. Lindsey stood up and stumbled slightly.

"I'm going to get the grill started!"

"You were serious? About inviting those guys?"

"Well, sort of. I mean, we have to eat at some point. If they want to hang out and get a bite to eat, that's fine by me. After all, they were good sports earlier. Don't worry, I'm not going to do anything stupid. I just think it would be polite and besides, it would be fun to have them hang out for a bit."

Kelly offered to get the grill started while Lindsey and I went to the kitchen and gathered the food. When we went back out to the yard, we saw that Kelly was completely surrounded by the three roofers and they were helping her light the grill.

"You guys sticking around for some food? You're more than welcome!"

They quickly agreed to stay for a while. Everything was casual and the guys were all very nice. We talked and found out that two of them were home from college and roofing was their summer job. The one with the nicest arms had just gotten out of the Navy and was going to be starting training at the Police Academy in another month. I tended to feel myself drawn to him more than the other guys. He was so much more interesting to talk to. He was a couple of years older than the others, a little closer to my own age. When everyone was done eating, Hunter, the Navy guy, told the others that he was ready to head home. They were involved in a drinking game with Kelly and Lindsey. To my surprise, Hunter offered to give me a ride home. I really wasn't sure what to say. I kind of wanted to hang out with Lindsey and Kelly, but something told me that maybe this guy really liked me. Maybe he would ask me out. I decided to be the good girl and see if it worked. I accepted his offer.

I gathered my clothes and purse. I left my swimsuit on and wrapped a towel around myself, rather than change. I looked back at my friends to say goodbye, but they barely noticed. I asked Hunter if he thought they would be all right with the guys and he assured me they would be fine. I had my doubts. Not because the boys would get out of hand, no, it was the drunken, horny girls I worried would do something crazy. As fun as it sounded over there, I knew they would be regretting something by morning and I didn't want anything to do with it. Especially if I wanted to show off my best behavior to this guy, Hunter. He just seemed like the nicest guy. I could easily picture Lindsey and Kelly starting a game of strip poker or something. Not the way to meet someone nice, but a nice way to meet someone!

Hunter and I walked over to his pickup truck and he actually opened the door for me. Right then and there, I knew he was someone I wanted on my radar. We talked about a few things, just getting a little information about one another. He told me about his four years in the Navy and how excited he was to have been accepted to the Police Academy. Inside I was bubbling with excitement, and it wasn't because of the alcohol. This was the kind of excitement you get when you come across someone with possibilities. He asked quite a bit about me, also. That said a lot. Usually, guys are all about themselves. They never ask much about you. When he stopped in front of my house, he paused for a minute, like he was trying to figure out what to say. Finally, he spoke.

"Would you mind if I asked you for your number? I would like it, if I could give you a call sometime. Maybe, we could go out and do something fun."

"Yeah, I think that would be really great!" The best part was that I really meant it. I reached in my purse and scratched around for a pen and paper. He picked up his phone and told me to tell him the number. He added me in to his contacts. I am such a dork sometimes. I didn't even think of that! He recited his phone number and I added his number to my phone, just in case.

Chapter Eight

Shakedown Cruise

I had to admit, I was pretty happy with how everything had gone so far with my experiments. Lindsey now had a new roof, and she was fully entertaining herself with a duo of hotties.

As far as Kelly's spell went, what can I say? I only urged Florian along. I can't help that his brand of doctor was a pecker checker. I had nothing to do with that. Besides, she was enjoying herself at Lindsey's bacchanalia. I only needed to hear back from Kim and Jennifer.

I had known Jennifer since I was a kid. She was our next door neighbor. She had moved up from Texas to Chicago and we hit it off immediately. She was the sweetest person I had ever met. I knew if I needed to talk to someone, she was there for me, always and unequivocally. A few years ago, she had enough of the long cold winters and moved back to Texas. She told me, she just couldn't take all the fucking snow anymore. She also thought the people in Chicago were nuts. There were days that I missed her so much, I was tempted to fly to Texas and drag her ass back. The only thing that stopped me, was that I knew she had a life there and she truly hated all things Chicago.

I didn't know for certain if she had gotten the cruise I had written for her, but if she did, she would be on it. I really wanted her to have a relaxing vacation. If anyone deserved it, it was Jennifer!

I crash landed on my couch, completely wiped out from too much sun and one too many drinks. I turned the TV on and caught the local news. Another cruise ship had broken down in the Gulf of Mexico. There was no power and no plumbing for the thousands of people stranded on it. They were gathered on the top decks and they looked more like refugees than happy or even remotely relaxed vacationers. *Oh shit, oh shit! Please don't let Jennifer be on that ship!* I repeated the mantra over and over in my head, hoping like hell to make it come true!

The news was showing a live video feed from a helicopter as it circled the enormous ship. I kept praying Jennifer wasn't on that thing. They seemed to be focusing on one woman who was near the stern of the ship. She had on one of those giant sombreros that people buy for souvenirs in Acapulco or Cancun. Her arms flailed about wildly, as if she were hailing the helicopter crew. The camera zoomed in closer and there she was, my BFF Jennifer, in all of her glory. She was the woman in the sombrero. She was mouthing something. I was busily thanking God that they couldn't pick up what she was saying. If they did, they would have had to censor the entire diatribe of Texas tinged profanity that was trailing off the back of the ship.

I shut the TV off and held my face in my hands. I couldn't stand seeing her there stuck in hell on that floating disaster of a ship. The whole thought made me sick. This spell wasn't going well at all. How could I be to blame? Sure, I had gotten Jennifer on a cruise ship, with the best of intentions, I might add. It isn't my fault that those poorly maintained, barnacle encrusted, floating coffins are engineering disasters that are just waiting to happen! Not to mention, they are teeming with every virus the tropics can contribute to the plague-ridden atmosphere and vermin infested interior. Ugh! Why did I choose to send her on a cruise of all things? I guess that's why the warning was written under the desk. Fine, I'll take the blame on that one too.

I started thinking about Kim. Surely, she must have hit it big on the game show. I really couldn't think of any negative consequences to getting a little pile of cash and a new car. I hadn't heard from Kim in a while, so I decided to give her a call.

"Hello, Kim? It's Leigh."

"Hello." Her voice was flat and listless. I cringed, wondering what could have possibly went wrong.

"Wow, you sure sound down, what's wrong?"

"Well, not so much *down* as I am sore. Plus, I'm on muscle relaxers right now, so I feel like I'm in a scuba diving suit under a hundred feet of water."

"Holy hell! What happened?"

"Remember, I told you about how I was practicing for that game show? It paid off. I kicked some serious ass on that game. I won twelve thousand dollars and a brand new Mustang."

"That's fantastic!"

"It *was* fantastic. Until I picked up the car. Did you know, that you have to pay all of the taxes and fees before you can pick up the car?"

"No, I never thought about it. I just assumed the winners got the keys and drove it home."

"Nope. They subtract taxes from the cash winnings, also. So in the end, I handed over whatever was left of the cash, plus a few thousand dollars in order to get the car."

"Oh wow! I'm sorry! How did you get hurt?"

"I had just picked up the car. I got on the freeway and made it only a few miles. Out of nowhere, something had fallen and landed right on top of my car from an overpass. You'll never guess what it was, so I'll just tell you. It was a pile of pig guts. A truck from Wisconsin, carrying a load of pig guts fresh from a slaughterhouse had taken the curve too sharp and the trailer flipped over. I guess the entire overpass was knee deep in the gory, smelly mess. Some speeding jack wad slammed into the pile of guts and gore. That caused a whole shit load of it to fly up into the air before falling on to the highway below, just as I was coming out of the overpass. It was an instant shock because I never saw it coming, and I had no idea what it was. One second I was a happy camper thrilled with my new car and the next-blood and guts everywhere."

"Oh my God!"

"Yeah, I said a whole lot more than oh my God! Imagine, Leigh, suddenly your windshield gets slammed by a pile of bloody, smelly guts out of nowhere. I can't even begin to describe the shock I was in. It scared the shit out of me. I thought I killed someone! I don't even know what happened. I think I slammed on the brakes out of instinct. My brand new Mustang! I got hit from behind and shoved right into the barrier along the side of the highway. My poor, beautiful, brand new Mustang was totaled. Plus, I got whiplash and a few sprains."

"Wow. I am so sorry, even sorrier than you know."

"The real kick in the teeth is the fact that I didn't even get insurance on it. Of course the guy that hit me from behind didn't have any insurance either. Either way, I'm completely screwed because I junked my old car. I ended up winning the whole game show, but I am out about two thousand bucks, my old car, and a sore neck. I would have been better off, had I never gone on the show to begin with."

My phone was making a noise to notify me of an incoming call. I told Kim that I was sorry, once more, and then tried to catch the other call. I clicked over a moment too late and nobody was there. The missed call notice showed that Kelly had called. There was a voicemail from her and I played it back. All I heard was a bunch of screaming in the background. I was terrified that something had happened. I mean really? How could I not be, after what happened to Jennifer and Kim? I tried calling her back several times with no luck. I tried Lindsey's number. No luck. I wondered if Hunter would have the number to the other roofers. Maybe he could call them and see what was going on. I quickly dialed his number with the hope that he didn't think I was a raving lunatic.

"Hunter? Hi, it's Leigh. You gave me a ride home earlier."

"Hi! I was just thinking about you."

Awe, he was thinking about me. I'd have to hold on to that thought for later. Thanks to me, my friends could be in real trouble.

"Umm, that's great, but I think there's a problem over at my friend Lindsey's house, where you guys were working today. I got a voicemail from her, but it was just- well, it sounded a lot like screaming. I tried calling back to both her and Kelly, but there was no answer on either of their phones. Normally, I would drive over there and check things out, but I don't have my car here with me and I'm really worried. I don't know those guys, and the girls were doing a lot of drinking. How well do you know them?"

I didn't want to tell him what a shitty witch I was, or what was going on with all of my experiments. I'm not even going to mention, how I had inadvertently placed all of my friends and family into disastrous scenarios. I wanted him to like me, not run away screaming!

"Oh, I seriously doubt there would be a problem. I've worked with Luke and Derek long enough to know that they are good guys. They're both related to the owner of the roofing company, too. I have their numbers, let me make a few calls and I'll call you right back."

"OK. Thanks, Hunter."

I paced around the living room in an attempt to calm my nerves. Luna came up to me and was being unusually sweet. She rubbed her tail against the side of my leg and then jumped up onto my writing desk. It was almost as if she wanted me to write.

"Sorry, Luna. I don't have anything left to write about tonight." After hearing about all of the disasters I caused, there was no way that I was going to write anymore until I found out what the hell was going on!

I had been tempted earlier to write a nice date for Hunter and me, but with the way things are going, who knows what kind of disaster would await us. Besides, I genuinely liked him. I wanted to see if a natural relationship could develop on its own. You know, the kind with zero supernatural influence or interference!

My phone rang. Thankfully, it was Hunter calling me back. I had started to wear a hole in my carpet from pacing back and forth. I was completely sick with worry.

"Well, no answer from any of them. I'm going to head over to Lindsey's place and see for myself what's going on. They probably aren't even there anymore, but I'd rather be safe than sorry. Would you mind coming along, so it doesn't seem too weird for me to be showing up alone at this hour? The last thing I want to do is end up getting hauled into the police station for a misunderstanding."

"Sure. How long before you get here?"

"I'll be there in about ten minutes or so. I'll see you then."

I was beyond grateful for Hunter. My car was still sitting over at Lindsey's. Sure, I suppose that I could have called the police, but I really didn't have anything to go on. I really didn't want to cause any trouble for anyone. What was I going to tell them? I cast a few less than fortunate magic spells that went awry on my other friends. Now I'm worried about these two because of an odd voicemail and a lot of alcohol? They'd lock me up quicker than I could blink. Just for the record, my idea of a relaxing vacation had nothing to do with padded walls and a straitjacket! That is unless Vlad could be there with me… oh wait, that bitch killed him!

I quickly threw on a pair of shorts, a tank top, and my favorite sandals. By the time I was ready, Hunter was knocking at the door. I couldn't help but notice how nice he looked, now that he had showered and changed. Maybe I didn't appreciate the full quality of his hunkiness in my drunken stupor earlier in the day, but now- whew, I appreciated! The spark was definitely a little more than ignited. I felt like my body might internally combust from the smile he sent my way.

I hadn't noticed that his eyes were the lightest, most amazing shade of blue. His blonde, thick hair was begging for my fingers to run through it while he did naughty things to me. His full pouty lips were absolutely made for sin. Suddenly, I remembered the way he looked with his shirt off on Lindsey's roof. Fuck me, I literally started to drool.

When I was finally done making an ass of myself and checking Hunter out, we headed for his truck. I had to give him brownie points for trying not to laugh at my not so discreet ogling.

We zipped over to Lindsey's and knocked on her front door. There was no answer. We could hear the music blaring loudly from inside. It sounded like her tiny home had been transformed into a bar. We made our way to the back of the house and found the door unlocked. Hunter led the way. The kitchen was empty, but when we got to the living room, the scene was pretty much what I had envisioned.

"Whoohoo! Two more for strip poker!" Yelled a very topless and very drunk Kelly.

Lindsey still had both parts of her swimsuit on, but the guys were down to their underwear. One of them was standing in front of Lindsey. I guessed that he must have been the loser of that hand, since Lindsey was slowly tugging at the waist band of his underwear, in a vain attempt to strip them off. The guy was quite drunk and trying to dance in front of her.

"Well, Hunter what do we do? Should we leave them? I mean, they're all adults here and from the looks of it, quite consenting." I was at a complete loss for words. I wanted to see if I could keep Hunter's attention long enough to hold a conversation as Kelly's massive milkers bounced freely around the room. Let's face it, she definitely did *NOT* get passed over in the boob department. If there was anything on my body that I would have wished differently, it was to have Kelly's boobs, instead of my own. Hers were spectacular! This was an unexpected test for Hunter. I hope he passed with flying colors.

"You're right, as stupid as they all look right now, you're right. I'm

going to take the keys to the truck
they brought here and offer them a
ride. I can't make them leave, but I'm
not letting them drive. Hey guys, you
know you have to be at the job site by
six in the morning? How about loading
up into the work truck and I'll drive
you home?"

I was pleasantly surprised when he
acted as if Kelly were fully clothed,
nothing impressive there. I was still
gaping over the display of her bared
rack!

"Awww," Lindsey protested. "It was
just getting good, too! I was finally
going to get to see Derek's goods!"

Luke agreed with Hunter and slowly
put his jeans and shirt back on.
Lindsey quickly grabbed the elastic
waistband of her vanquished card
player.

"Not so fast, you still have to
pay up."

To our surprise, she reached her
hand down into his shorts and grabbed
ahold of his assets. She pulled his
shorts down with the other hand
revealing what she had gotten ahold of.

"Nice!" She gave it a few strokes
and then smacked his ass and told him
to get dressed.

"I wonder how much of this she will remember in the morning." I said to Hunter.

"Oh, I'm sure she will have a vague memory of it."

"Leigh, the work truck is a cargo truck. The guys can climb in the back and I'll drive you home, if you'd like."

"I would say I'm sober enough to drive, but I don't take any chances, even though it's been about four hours since I've had a drink. So, I'll take you up on your offer."

Lindsey laid down on the couch and was already asleep. Kelly slumped into a chair next to her.

"Hold on, I just want to cover these girls up. I cannot wait to call them early tomorrow morning." I went into Lindsey's room and took some of the fluffy blankets from her bed and spread them over the now snoring beauties. Next, I set their ringers to the most annoying ring tones I could find. Oh, and I turned the volume up all the way.

Hunter herded the two young roofers out the front door and ushered them into the back of the truck. He rolled down the door and latched it shut, so none of them could stumble back out. "You all should probably sit down before you fall down." He yelled to the boys.

Once again, he held the passenger door open for me, but this time he took my hand and helped me up into the cab, which was much higher off the ground than his truck was. The truck bounced and creaked away into the night, accompanied by the groaning protesters in the back. Apparently, they failed to heed the warning of sitting down.

"Thank you, for helping out. I would invite you in when I get home, but I think you have some special cargo to deliver."

"Yeah, these guys are all staying at the boss's house. I bet every one of them will be late to the job in the morning."

"Yeah, well, I think we got there just in time. It looked like they were about to get a little too crazy. I swear that I've never seen Lindsey or Kelly act like that before." Which was a complete lie. There was one time that was equally as bad as, or perhaps even worse than what we walked in on tonight. The incident happened at a bachelorette party we were all invited to. The party featured two male strippers and since it was being held in someone's house, there were absolutely no rules.

We all had our hands on the goods that night! Well, we almost had our hands on the goods. I was busily stuffing one dollar bills into this stripper's skimpy little G-string. Kelly came over and pulled his cock out and tried to stick it in my face. Sorry, but I really don't have any interest in a cock that makes a living by sticking it in every horny woman or maybe horny guy, in the city. Sorry, but that's just not my cup of tea. I'm all for having a fun time with the girls, but I have to draw the line at public sex acts with strangers.

The bride to be was the worst. She actually gave an oral performance… in front of all of us. Somebody recorded it on their phone, which was a complete breech of etiquette and probably blackmail material for later in life.

I was pretty sure Lindsey was about to reenact the same scene with the young roofer tonight. I really had to wonder what the hell had gotten into them. I knew, I had nothing to do with that. No, I think that was just two young, single, and very drunk women surrounded by shirtless studs. And hormones, let's not forget about those little bastards. Lindsey attended an all-female Catholic school and college when she was growing up. I know first-hand that she looks for any opportunity to make up for what could have been massive amounts of juvenile delinquent behavior, with a side of wild girl syndrome. Not everything in life is sprinkled with magic, stupidity frequently and easily trumps witchcraft.

Hunter stopped the truck in front of my place. I thanked him once more for the lift. The guy was just too nice. It was killing me! He's everything I would expect to find in the best of my best book boyfriends. He asked me once more about getting together soon. How could I refuse?

"Hey, Leigh, I just want you to know that tonight doesn't count."

It took me a minute to comprehend what he meant. "Oh, I fully agree! I'm looking forward to spending time with someone other than my insane friends and psychotic cat."

"We better do it soon, though. I'll be heading to the academy in less than four weeks. How about we get together on Thursday, if you're free that is? I have the day off. I started shortening my work hours, so I can get more time to work out and do some studying for the academy. It's a great opportunity and I really want to graduate as close to the top as I can."

"Thursday would be perfect. I'm completely free all day and evening, too. Just give me a call to let me know what time you want to get together and we'll go from there." Of course, I wasn't free at all. I had a veterinarian appointment in the afternoon for Luna's annual exam and a book club meeting in the evening. Neither of those were as important as the prospect of a potentially awesome date with a man that seemed to have a lot of book boyfriend qualities. If it would have been Carl on the other hand, I would have chosen to go to the book club meeting. It had become pretty stale lately, since one of the new members acted like a goddamn dominatrix with her pushy attitude and pleather skirts.

I knew the next thing on my agenda was to find out how long the Chicago Police Academy course would be. Hopefully short and sweet. Wait, strike that. Something could go terribly wrong.

Chapter Nine

Witchcraft.com

I had a couple of days before my expected date with Hunter. By now, I had almost given up on Vlad. Almost. I had already gone back and started reading the series from the first book. I missed the magic of a good story. I wasn't quite ready to attempt a resurrection of Vlad, until I had honed my witchcraft. When I pondered the idea, I realized that perhaps I needed to learn more about witchcraft, if I expected to gain control of it. Another thing, I figured I had at least a few days left to change the outcome of my parents' weekend.

Other than throw my friends and family into hellish situations, what else could I do? I started by delving into information with my research partner. If you've never researched "witchcraft" on the internet, you are in for a real treat. The historical facts are buried under steaming manure piles of completely useless garbage. I mean, think about it. Don't you think, if it was as easy as throwing together a few herbs and saying some silly words to accomplish whatever you wanted, everyone would be doing it? It seemed like everyone was into some new age spiritual revival, I had completely and thankfully missed out on.

I'm pretty open minded, so when I came across one of these tried and true internet fueled magic spells, I decided to give it a try. The spell was called Wisdom. It promised that the witch would be able to make wise decisions with her or his power. Now, I normally ignore most of *that* kind of stuff on the internet, but wisdom is something I desperately needed right about now. Especially, if I planned to play around with altering someone's future. I had to be smart. Witchy smart. There was one more thing that gave the spell some validity. The website included images of the original medieval magic book. Of course, most of it was in Latin and some Greek. The rest appeared to be written in a strange alchemist's code.

Now, like any classic witch spell, it required a number of ingredients. Some of these things were pretty easily found in any spice rack. Bay leaf, saffron, and sea salt. It would be more difficult to get my hands on the five drops of goose blood and the cow's tears. A quick check of my kitchen and just as I suspected, I had everything but the goose blood and cow tears. Do cows even cry?

Time to call on my irrational and insane friends to get my car back and see if they wanted to help me whip up a batch of wisdom. I let Kelly's phone ring until I reached her voicemail and then I tried Lindsey's. They were probably still sprawled out like road-kill, right where I left their drunken asses. Finally, after another try to Kelly's phone, she picked up.

"Ahhhhhhrrrr," she both growled and moaned. "What do you want? I'm busy dying here."

"You guys need to come pick me up. We have some shopping to do. Well, not so much of a shopping trip as it is a scavenger hunt."

"What the hell? Really? Does it have to be today?"

"Yes, it does. Now get yourselves together, I'll be waiting!"

Almost an hour and a half later, Kelly slinked through my door. "Holy hell, Kel! You look like dog meat!"

"Thanks for the compliment, Leigh. I tried. I really did, but this is the best it's going to get today." Kelly feebly waived her hand over her face and hair.

"Where's Lindsey?"

"She is hurting- bad."

I laughed and asked Kelly what she remembered from the previous night's strip poker game. Like any good friend, I had to tease the hell out of her. When these opportunities arise with loved ones, you must strike quick and hard! "So, do you remember the strip poker game?"

"Ugh! You saw that? It's all pretty fuzzy still. We were just having fun. They're nothing but college guys. They were cool about it, and to be honest, it was a bit reminiscent of being back in college. For me at least."

"Yeah, I didn't see *all* of it. I walked in right as Lindsey was about to strip the one guy completely naked. I interrupted her little show."

"Speaking of guys. Where did you skip off to with Mr. Arms? Don't think for a minute that we didn't notice your little disappearing act!"

"Mr. Arms, by the way is Hunter. He is probably the nicest guy that I've met in a very long time. We actually have a date Thursday night. You see, I have something called self-control, unlike the two of you. You two acted like it was your first night of freedom from a women's correctional institution." Kelly simply rolled her eyes, which was probably a bad idea considering the fact that she still smelled like a brewery. The room probably started to spin on her again.

"Pffft. You forget, I know all of your secrets. Besides, I'm happy you have a date. Maybe I'll get Luke's number and give him a call. I'm pretty sure, I saw Derek writing his number on Lindsey's thigh with a sharpie. Anyway, now that I'm here, what exactly are we doing today?"

"Witchcraft! More precisely, a magic spell that will hopefully give me better control over using my newfound witchy powers. I found out some pretty interesting things about my desk and I need to find a way to tame it."

"Like?" Kelly prompted.

"It has a message written in Latin under the drawer. *Cave quid dicis, quando, et cui,* and translated it means, *beware of what you say, when, and to whom.* I also contacted the old bitch who gave it to me. I had to practically twist her into a knot to tell me anything about it. She told me the desk was very old and came from Massachusetts!"

"Woohoo! Massachusetts! Lucky you!" Kelly was dripping with sarcasm. "My cousin married a guy who came from Massachusetts, and let me tell you, there is nothing magical about that son of a bitch."

"No! My desk is very old and it belonged to a witch!"

"He IS old and I've heard that his ex IS a real witch." Kelly said in a lifeless tone. "All right, just kidding, Leigh. That's actually a pretty cool story. So, you think that you've gained this long forgotten witch's power?"

"Exactly. I know I did."

"Let me guess. You sicced Florian the troll boy on me. Didn't you?"

"Yes, but only to have him call you back. It ended there."

"Well, then you *are* a witch all right! That's just one word and not the word that I would choose to use, but hey, my game isn't quite up to par today."

"Anyway, I want to try some other magic. Not the magic that requires the desk. I want to see if some of that power rubbed off on me in other ways. Enough of it to at least perhaps try some good old fashioned magic spell stuff. I found this spell on the internet…"

"Stop right there. Internet? You found it on the internet? You do realize that some fourteen year old probably made that up. Ugh! This is going to be bad. Anything that follows the statement, I found this spell on the internet is not going to have a good ending!"

I opened the web page and pointed out the medieval manuscript. It was after all the supposed reference of my wisdom spell. I defiantly pointed it out to Kelly.

"See, Kel, this is something that is at least based on a real book of magic. I'm not saying that it will work, but I think it could be fun to give it a try."

"Wow, you are seriously embracing this whole witch thing. Aren't you?"

I suppose Kelly was right about that. Why shouldn't I? The first thing we had to find was goose blood.

"Of course I am. Now, where do you think we will find goose blood?"

"Simple, Leigh. Haha! I crack myself up!"

When I looked at her like a lost deer in the headlights, she finally took a moment to elaborate… yay for me, more people messing with my name!

"SimpLeigh- Simply, get it? Find a butcher shop that sells goose or geese to cook."

"Oh my God, you're such a dork! Gee, that sounds good, if you live in the time of Charles Dickens you might have a shot. Honestly, when is the last time you saw goose meat in the grocery store? Maybe if we could score an invite to the Jeffrey Dahmer house for Hanukkah, they could hook us up. Other than that, you aren't likely to find any place in Chicago where they are hacking apart a live goose in the back room."

"That's it, Leigh! You just figured out where to get one!"

"What? Serial killer school?"

"No. You said Hanukkah. So what about calling a kosher butcher? Don't they have to butcher geese a certain way? Maybe a small kosher butcher shop will sell or give you some goose blood?"

I don't know, I think the butchery takes place in a sterile plant or facility in Wisconsin or someplace, kosher. Besides, the whole idea of kosher meat is to get rid of the blood. It's not like they save it to supply the local witchcraft covens or hobbyists, and even if they did, what am I supposed to say? Hi, I'm a newbie witch and I need some goose blood for a spell."

"Fine, we can go to the city park and shank some poor unsuspecting goose or we can call a butcher. While we are at it, we'll see about cow's tears. Maybe they cry before they sentence them to death."

Kelly and I were so busy with our snarky banter that we didn't realize Lindsey had stumbled through the door. She had quietly listened in on our conversation, trying desperately to figure out what the fuck we were talking about. "Safeway. They sell goose livers. I'm pretty sure they are dripping with it."

"See. That's why we love you, Lindsey. You're always thinking. Well, when you're not in the middle of a drunken orgy. Now, cow's tears. Any suggestions?"

"Got it. All we have to do is go by the petting zoo that we had the students go to last year. Cows, bulls, calves, pigs, you name it. We'll corner one of the cows and relate our lousy love lives to her. You can guarantee we will get sympathy tears." Lindsey seemed to be on a roll with the answers. Maybe, she should be hung over more often.

"With the exception of Leigh. Do you remember that roofer guy with the arms, Lindsey?"

"Oh yeah. Very fuckable. And, Leigh, we noticed that you two snuck away from the party."

"First, I want to clear up a few things. We didn't sneak anywhere. I announced loud and clear that Hunter was giving me a ride home. That's all that happened until I needed to call him, so we could go back to your so-called party and save you from becoming the internet hand-job queen."

Lindsey was silenced. She didn't remember! Time to pounce, strike fast and hard. Remember?

"Oh yeah, Lindsey, you may not remember. Strip poker? Kelly were topless. You had one guy in front of you and he was down to his skivvies. I came in just in time as you were shamelessly wrangling his snake free."

"Hmmm, well then, I blame you, Leigh, you and your naughty little witchcraft. Kelly spilled the beans on what you've been up to and that's precisely why I couldn't wait to see what you were doing today. By the way, next time you want to magically hook me up, please remember something. I'm not as experienced at being a slut as some people." She nodded to Kelly. "And dammit, make me sober next time, because I sure wish I could remember the whole snake part. I've got nothing. Was his package big? Small? Microscopic? These really are details a woman *needs* to remember, damn it!"

Thankfully, good friends transcend complete and utter insults such as these and we had a good laugh. I couldn't break it to Lindsey that her lewd conduct was completely of her own accord.

We eventually made it into Kelly's car and headed for the children's petting zoo. The brightly painted little barns and animal shaped playground equipment reminded me of how nice it was not to be responsible for twenty five little hellions trying out novel ways to end up as plaintiffs in a personal injury lawsuit.

We strolled in past a variety of foul smelling beasts, and Kelly made an observation in her typical fashion.

"Oh God, can you imagine what it must have been like on Noah's Ark? Seriously. Forty days trapped in a floating barn full of seasick people and parasite ridden animals wading around in their own filth? I can barely stomach being around these things when they are supposedly cared for professionally."

"Yeah, I'm thinking you would have been one of the people listed as *persona non grata*, left to clamber up the last tall tree." Lindsey remarked.

"I don't think those heels would help her much for tree climbing, anyway." I had to chime in.

"Oh, and how would you two get onboard? I'm thinking you could easily pass as a pair of jackasses."

"Touché, Kelly." Lindsey responded.

"Hey! There's your cow!" Lindsey leaned out over the fence as far as she could and pursed her lips. She made some obscene smacking sounds that apparently raised the animal's curiosity. Lindsey stepped onto the fence's bottom rung and leaned further out, in an attempt to call the cow over to us. "Here cow-cow, come on, who's a good girl?" Kelly plucked some nearby dandelions and handed them to Lindsey. She waved the limp wanna-be flowers, trying to entice the cautious bovine.

Now, this was one of those times when you just know, while it was happening, that a human was about to plummet into the world of the cow. In this case, the human got a little help over the fence. We were pretty close to the exit of one of the psychedelically painted mini-barns. Just as Lindsey flapped her dandelion bouquet wildly in the air, a herd of screaming tiny children broke through the rainbow emblazoned door and charged toward us in a surreal jailbreak scene.

There is always the one kid who is about a foot taller than the others. This group had a couple of them that were plowing through their daycare mates, as if they were berserkers on a bloodthirsty rampage. The wall of little bodies pushed against the fence, causing it to lean into the cow pen. Lindsey squealed and hit the muddy ground with a very wet plop. The children instantly halted and faced the pen.

Their screams and laughs couldn't drown out the stream of obscenities that spewed from Lindsey's mouth with incredible speed. Kelly and I gaped at the scene before us, trying desperately to contain our laughter. Lindsey stood up. She was covered head to toe in cow dung and mud. Finally, the last of several creative uses for the word *fuck* passed her lips. Her problem was that she had a mouthful of cow manure-tinged mud that she was trying to spit out while she cussed. This worked to her favor, as the kids probably thought she was some crazed woman doing a Daffy Duck imitation in a foreign language. "Theptafuckapthh, bleh thpuck! Thpuck! Moh my thpuckin thbod!"

The cow seemed momentarily unnerved by the whole ordeal. It must have recovered quickly because with the very next moo, it shamelessly defecated right beside Lindsey. The boys' cheers raised to a fever pitch at the sight and sickening plopping sounds. Lindsey slogged up to the fence and started to crawl out between the rails. As she made it through the fence, the cow had followed her and placed its head between the rails. I seized the opportunity to examine her eyes. I wasn't sure if they classified as tears or mucous, but there was something definitely leaking in the corner of the cow's eye. I scratched her neck and pulled out the small Ziploc bag and a Popsicle stick I had brought along. An elementary teacher always comes prepared for any situation. I carefully scooped off the goo and slipped it into the baggie.

Finally, we had achieved our goal and made it out to the parking lot. Kelly had a few beach towels and several gallons of water in the trunk of her car. We stood with the towels stretched out to cover Lindsey while she stripped off the clothes that were covered in cow shit and mud. She stuffed them into a plastic grocery store bag and tossed them into the trunk. Lindsey quickly dumped several gallons of water over her head and limbs in an attempt to rid herself of the filth. When she was finished, she wrapped her hair and body with a couple of the fluffy beach towels and climbed into the back seat of Kelly's car. She grumbled the entire way home while Kelly and I tried our best to stop laughing.

We made a quick stop at the grocery store on the way back to my apartment. I ran in to purchase a goose liver from the deli. The deli manager explained they do not sell it. They only have it to make a gourmet pate. I begged him for a small amount, telling him that I was a chef and I had been suddenly inspired to create a new goose-liver pate. He handed it over to me for free in an apparent feeling of comradeship with a fellow goose-liver pate aficionado.

The girls dropped me off and headed back to Lindsey's. I was excited to try some real old-fashioned spell casting. Luna greeted me at the door, as if she knew what I was up to and the look on her face was quite condescending. She zipped away and leapt up to my desk. There wasn't too much to prepare. According to the web page, I needed to print out the diagram of a pentagram surrounded with alchemist symbols. I didn't know this before, but apparently what real witches used in the past were bowls for mixing their ingredients. Not big cast iron cauldrons, just bowls.

I scrounged through my meager collection of Tupperware and Corelle dishes. I found a generic plastic salad bowl with a missing lid. It would have to do. After all, the instructions required me to write a magic spell in the bottom of the bowl, and I'd be damned if I was going to use my good dishes.

Luna stared intently. I didn't have any candles suitable for witchcraft, you know, black tapers or the like. I did have a large pillar candle that was a gift from my mother. I looked at the cellophane wrapped label, *Morning Rain.* I had never lit the candle, not because I liked the way it looked, but because I was afraid to smell Morning Rain throughout my apartment. To me, those words conjured up thoughts of the scent of a thousand worms dying on the sidewalk. And, I might add, I have a real problem with the reason for all of those worms. I imagine that somewhere deep in the earth, as the falling rain penetrates the inner sanctum of Wormtown, their Jim Jones style worm leader makes an announcement that the end of the world is at hand. OK, maybe not at hand in the worm sense, but perhaps with wormaggedon imminent, they are all ordered to go up to the surface where they lay prostrate in front of traffic, pedestrians, and hungry birds.

The smell, oddly reminiscent of dead worms on a rainy spring morning, hung in the air of my dimly lit room. I took my sharpie marked salad container and centered it on the paper. Luna jumped down and sat next to me. The herbal ingredients were tossed in and I read the magic incantation as I spun the bowl. Now, on to the nasty goose blood. I opened the clear plastic deli container and took a small spoonful of the red liquid and dripped it in. Next, I scraped Betsy's eye boogers into the mix. It was disgusting. I was even more disgusted when I saw Luna chowing down on raw goose liver.

I waited and waited, but nothing happened. I suppose, I had hoped for a sign that the spell had worked. A puff of smoke or an enlightening feeling, something – anything, but I got a whole lot of nothing. I blew the candle out and threw away the bowl full of yuck. Luna disappeared into my bedroom and left me alone. At least I gave it a try, and I really did have a good time at Lindsey's expense that day. The only thing I could really think about though was Hunter. I was looking forward to seeing him. A real, big girl date. Yay me!

Chapter 10

It's a Date!

I woke up early and felt thoroughly excited. I wondered what Hunter would have in mind for our date. I really didn't know that much about him. Probably a matinee, maybe dinner. It didn't matter to me, though. I didn't even bother to get my car from Lindsey's house. I hopped in the tub, shaved my legs, moved on to my nails, and then plucked the stray hairs from every pluckable part of my body. Finally the phone rang, it was Hunter. He told me that he would pick me up at noon and to expect a fun day. I'm pretty certain my heart skipped a few beats with the anticipation only a first date with potential can bring.

Like any normal, slightly psychotic woman that is trying desperately to impress a man, I tore through my closet like the Tasmanian devil. It's hard to pick out the perfect outfit, when you have absolutely no idea what the occasion is. After ten different outfits, I finally settled on a light pink sweater, a pair of white capris, and my favorite silver sandals. My hair, well that was another story. Should I leave it down? Should I pull it up? I finally decided to leave it down and take a clip with me, in case I wanted to pull it up at any time.

My mind was completely occupied with getting ready for my date that I barely thought about witchcraft. I had to admit to myself, at least, I was pretty upset the internet spell turned out to be a total bust. It led me to the realization that Kelly was right, no real magic would be out on the internet for anyone to use. In any case, I think I looked about as cute as I could possibly be.

Luna jumped up onto the back of my couch and looked out the window. Her tail twitched from side to side as she eyed up her next victim. When Hunter knocked on the door, I paused and counted to ten before I opened it. I didn't want him to know I had actually been standing by the door waiting for him. How desperate would that look?

"Hi, Hunter! Come on in." I held the door open and as Hunter walked in, Luna walked up to him and rubbed her body against his leg. Her tail wrapped around his ankle and she made a small noise. That little tramp! My cat was actually flirting with my would-be boyfriend. God knows that I would have loved to rub up against his leg and purr!

"Hi, Leigh and hi Leigh's cat."

"Wow! This is amazing. I've never seen her take to anyone like this before. She's normally an anti-social and violent psychopath." I looked at Hunter and noticed how nice he looked again. He wore a very nice, blue button down dress shirt, jeans, and brown leather shoes. His hair was short, but not buzzed like you see so many guys do. Working in the sun made his blonde hair look almost golden. His bright blue eyes were a stark contrast against his tanned skin. I could easily find myself lost in his eyes. I looked at his clean shaven face and the way he filled out his shirt. I blushed a little when I remembered how muscular and sexy he looked that afternoon working on Lindsey's roof.

"What's her name?"

"Who's name?" I had completely lost the conversation.

"Your cat's name."

"Oh, sorry. That's Luna. We have what you would call a very dysfunctional relationship, although it has been getting better lately for some reason." Which was absolutely true.

Ever since I started playing with magic, Luna began acting different. Almost as if she were more interested in being with me. Huh, I'd have to file that information away for later. This wasn't the time to bring up my witchy experiments to Hunter.

"Good name! I like that. So, are you ready to go out and have some fun?"

"Sure! What do you have in mind?"

"Well, this time of day there isn't a whole lot going on. I was thinking that since it's a nice day, we could head over to the little amusement park. The one with the go-kart track and mini golf course."

"Sounds fun!" For once, I didn't have to lie too much. It sounded like a lot of fun and I was really looking forward to spending time with him!

Once again, he held the door of his truck open for me. I have to admit that it is a very sweet and romantic thing to do, but for a moment, I worried that he might be in the market for an old-fashioned girlfriend. Maybe he hoped for a meek and mild girl? Then again, we had met when I was in a bikini and half drunk, so that couldn't possibly be the case.

It was a picture perfect summer day and it was even better because I was out doing something with Hunter. I was nervous about one thing. Mini-golf. I hate it. Well, I only hate it because I completely suck at it. I detest the full size version of the game even more. The sight of the course's sheet metal lighthouse and plastic gorilla summoned up a few traumatic childhood memories. When I was young, every summer my parents would take us up to Wisconsin for a week long adventure at Yogi Bear Campground. We stayed in one of the small log cabins, because as my father said, "What, they expect us to stay in a tent? We're from Skokie for God's sake." He said it as if people should excuse us from any expectations that we would ever truly leave our urbanized shells.

We always played the campground's mini-golf course on the first day. It was invariably hot, humid, and filled with children as miserable as my sister and I. It seemed like it was also the norm for frazzled parents to bring your most ADHD afflicted children for mini-golf therapy on the same day. Those parents were literally hanging onto their sanity by a hair. Every so often, a child would flail on the ground in some horrendous tantrum, as if they were possessed by every demon they could squeeze into their sweaty little heads. The most at-risk parents would confront the convulsing little monster, not with the Roman Catholic Rite of Exorcism, but with a complete psychotic break. The screaming imp was no match for a mother yelling a verbal tirade that would make Satan himself cower in fear. I always wondered why they thought it would help the situation by recalling every single transgression, real or perceived, the child had committed in the past two years.

So you had *that* to set the tone for your golf game. My father would get so upset. He thought these incidents destroyed our pace, or as I believed it to be, our spiraling descent into dysfunctional family hell. In an effort to expedite his nine-hole path to mini-golf fame, he would join in the fray by yelling at the parents to "go screw up your lives some other place. I paid good money to be here." I wondered, did he mean as a paying customer, he should be able to screw up his family with speed, unencumbered by the mental carnage going on around him? He would turn on us, determined to showcase us as model obedient children who were completely subservient to his newly founded dictatorship. No praise, accolades, or support. No, it was only impatient criticism laced with sarcasm. "Hurry up, we don't have all week for this! What are you doing? Just hit the ball!"

Needless to say, mini-golf wasn't anything that I wanted to partake in, but I didn't want Hunter to think I was dragging around a baggage cart full of weird hang-ups. We went to the small stand to pay our fee and get our golf clubs and balls. Hunter insisted that I take the first turn. The first hole looked nearly impossible. The green carpeting rolled out before me to create a snake shaped path. The course ahead went directly between the four limbs of a giant crouching plastic gorilla. I don't know why the gorilla was facing away from me. Perhaps intimidation was the latest in mini-golf design, as if bouncing a ball through a shifting mouse hole wasn't tough enough.

I set my bright pink ball on the little rubber pad and I had to lean down to use the club. I realized I had received the child size golf club. When I tried to set up an excuse before I even took my first pathetic swing, Hunter was happy to give me some assistance.

"Hunter, just so you know, I completely suck at this game."

"Don't worry about it, Leigh. I just thought it would be fun to play around. I didn't even grab a scorecard. Here, let me show you how to hold the putter." Hunter came up behind me and brought his big strong arms around to meet my hands on the club. "Now, hold your hands just like this." He moved my hands around to the correct grip and left his hands on mine. My entire body tingled from his touch. The whole scene was oddly erotic. "Next, swing the club back and don't squeeze your grip too tight, or you're likely to hit it too hard." He moved the club back to simulate the speed that I should use. I could feel his muscular chest up against my back. His head was leaning down so that the side of our faces were touching. "There, just like that. Now, let's hit this one together. Just keep your hands on the club and I'll hit it." Each time he brought that club back I could feel him against me, and I was suddenly and incredibly turned on by the way he was moving me. I didn't even realize that he said *he* would hit the ball.

We brought the club back and our combined forward swing was more like a major league baseball line drive. The little pink ball went airborne. A hollow thud ricocheted off the gorilla's left ass cheek. The ball came right back at us and I instinctively ducked. There was a sickening sound as the golf ball caught Hunter right in the forehead. I was so shocked that I spun around to see if he was all right. The only problem was that I had never let go of the club. If I had been in a martial arts tournament, I would surely have earned my black belt. The club came up and nailed Hunter right in the crotch with full force.

Hunter doubled over, his hands cupping what I imagined to be his mashed testicles. He dropped to the ground and tried to speak. To his credit, he didn't cuss at me or call me any names that would have been well deserved. "It's- OK... Leigh... I'm OK... I think- argh." With my mouth agape, I watched him writhing in pain, and then I noticed the contusion on his forehead swelling, as if a horn was about to burst out above his right eye. I finally meet a super-hot and nice guy and I fucking neutered him. It appeared that I may have caused some brain swelling as well. All in a single move. "Just give me a minute, Leigh."

I wanted to cry. Hunter tried to shake it off and slowly stood up. He

122

forced his hands away from his crotch, but was still leaning slightly forward. My eyes were now fixed on the red, bulbous lump on his head.

"See, just fine!"

"Hunter? I'm not so sure. You have a pretty big bump on your head."

"Aw, I'm sure it's nothing." He gave me a smile that seemed slightly forced. I could have sworn the thing was doubling in size before my very eyes.

"Well, how about we just give up on the golf? What do you say we just walk past those carnival games over there?" I wanted to get as far away from the mini-golf and the gorilla's ass as quickly as possible.

"Sure! That sounds safe… I mean, that sounds fun."

The first place we passed by was the shooting gallery. A colorful assortment of plush stuffed snakes, bears, monkeys, and other animals hung from the awning. I couldn't help it, I had to give a little squeeze to a plush orange and purple alligator. Hunter noticed that it had caught my attention. "How about I win one of those for you?"

He paid for his chance and with three shots from the cork gun he had three direct hits. He turned to me and handed me the prize, the psychedelic alligator. "Here you go. One grand prize. How about you give it a try?"

"I've never shot anything. Not even a cork gun."

"I'll show you!" Hunter threw down another five dollar bill and started to demonstrate how I should hold the little gun. I did my best to do it completely wrong.

"OK, I suck at this, too. I think you should come here and help me aim it."

I was pretty happy when my plan worked and much like he did with the mini golf lesson, he came from behind and showed me the best way to hold the little rifle. I took as long as possible, because I was trying to let him know I really liked him being close to me. Time to get a little flirt on.

"So, do I hold my head back, like this?" I leaned my head back against his chest. "And do I hold my hand back here?" I grabbed the stock close to my body and awkwardly waved the barrel.

"No, let me help you." In order to get to my hands, his arms came completely around me, as if he were holding me more than helping me with the gun. I leaned my head back a little and looked up. I was trying to build up the nerve to tell him that I wouldn't mind him holding me as long as he wanted. He surprised me. "This is kind of a nice way to spend an afternoon. I really like being with you, Leigh."

I laughed a little. "I was just thinking the same thing. Now, how do I make this thing shoot?"

By now, Hunter had probably realized I had sort of tricked him into holding me like this and he got his flirting skills on as well. "Well, you take one hand and grab around this part, then take just one finger and put it on the trigger. You want to touch it lightly and easily at first so it doesn't just shoot off unexpectedly." He took my hand in his and placed it on the curved grip of the stock. Slowly he wrapped my fingers around it. I was amazed at how he could touch my hands in such a sensual way. He took my index finger and placed it on the trigger. "Now, when you are ready, you need to squeeze it. Don't just go pulling on it. Squeeze it gently, at first."

"You are sassy! Are you sure? Just squeeze it? How about like this?" I wrapped my fingers around his index finger and stroked it. "Do you think that would work?"

We both started laughing at the exchange of corny innuendoes, and I inadvertently pulled the trigger as I lost control of the barrel, which pointed straight up. The cork shot out and bounced off of the metal rail above us and directly back down onto Hunter's head. "Thank God it was only a cork and not another golf ball!" Hunter said.

I went to set the cork gun down and accidentally caught the barrel on the angled metal support that held up the awning. I forcefully pulled it free and as I did, I pulled the retaining pin free. The awning slipped an inch and then froze in place. I breathed a sigh of relief and then just as I exhaled, it dropped. Hunter ducked just in time, or it would have caught him right in the teeth. He stood back up and laughed.

"You know, I never thought going out with you would be so danger-"

Then the entire awning frame came crashing down on the top of his head. I screamed and checked on him. Hunter sat with a blank stare, then he finished his sentence.

"Dangerous- or painful."

"This is my fault. I've never caused as much disaster as I did today."

"It's all right, Leigh. I'm thinking that I need to get some ice."

"Well, you do have that wounded look on your face. How about we head back to my place? I'll get you some ice and some ibuprofen."

Chapter 11

Reverse the Curse

Hunter accepted my offer and agreed to go back to my apartment. He handed me the keys and this time I helped him into his truck. When we got back to my apartment, I had him lie down on my couch. I went to get ice and ibuprofen. When I came back, I saw Luna curled up on his chest. I was a little jealous because that was the exact position I'd like to be in!

"Geez! I swear, she never acts like this, not even with me. How's your head? And everything else?"

"I'm sure the headache will go away soon." He gulped down the pills and put the icepack on his head. "We can still go out for dinner, later, if that's OK with you."

"Yeah, of course! But only if you're feeling well enough. You took a few good shots to the head today. Just relax and shut your eyes, if you need to." I left Hunter to recover while I thought about the events of the day. It was almost as if Hunter was under attack from my bad luck. Luna jumped down off of Hunter's chest and came over to the writing desk. She took one paw and swept a paper off of the desk. When I picked it up, I saw that it was the witch spell I had printed off the internet.

I picked it up and looked at the Latin incantation that I had recited for the spell. I simply assumed the spell was correct. Rookie witch mistake, I suppose. Something was going on with the way Hunter seemed to be cursed on our very first date. Apparently, Luna had a clue. I needed Lindsey. After all, she knew Latin. I took a picture of the spell with my phone and sent it to Lindsey with a request for her to translate it, if she could. I looked over at Hunter and he was asleep. I took my phone into the kitchen with Luna following me.

My phone rang within minutes. "So, are you worried about someone attacking you?"

"Huh? No, this is that spell for wisdom, but something went wrong."

"I'll say! It literally translates to, *Harm will befall the one who touches me.*"

"Dammit. So, I created a spell that would curse anyone that touches me? Fuck me! Seriously?"

"No, not likely. I strongly would suggest avoiding that pleasure, unless you want your lover to feel the wrath of whatever your newfound witchcraft can muster up."

"Do you think this is something I can reverse? The spell, I mean?"

"How would I know? I don't know the slightest thing about being a witch, let alone how spells work. I did see a TV show once where this witch had to read the spell backwards in order to reverse it, but I don't remember what else she had to do, or if it even worked for her."

I thanked Lindsey and after I hung up, I turned to Luna. "So, do you have any ideas how to fix this disaster?" Luna swatted my wormy smelling candle across the desk. "Light the candle?"

"Meow."

"OK, and then what? Do I read the spell backwards?"

"Meow, meow."

Could my cat really know what to do? Am I seriously contemplating listening to the advice of my cat? Well, why not? What else could possibly go wrong today? "OK, Luna. If I blow up the neighborhood or something, it's on you."

I lit the candle. The pungent odor filled the kitchen. I recited the spell backwards. The first time I reversed the order of the words and the second by clumsily trying to sound out the words with a reverse spelling.

"Let's hope this works, Luna. I don't want to be considered too dangerous to be around. I actually really like him."

"Meeeoww."

"I think you are saying that maybe I already am? Such a sassy little brat! Remind me again why I adopted you?"

I heard Hunter's voice calling out from the living room. "Did it rain or something? It smells like worms in here."

Luna and I went in to check on him. "Hey! Good to see you're still alive! Sorry about the smell. I lit a candle that is supposed to have a rain fresh smell, but I agree with you, it's much more like dying worms. Are you feeling any better?"

"Actually, I feel great! It's like my headache never happened."

I looked at his forehead and there was only a slight red mark now. "I'm completely ready to restart our date, if you are."

"Absolutely." Hunter sat up and Luna hopped into his lap. "I think we ought to head out to dinner, maybe it's a little early, but we haven't eaten all day. Italian sound good to you?"

"Sounds awesome! Am I dressed OK for the place that you have in mind?"

"You look perfect, Leigh."

"Just one thing, Hunter. You've got a small red spot on your forehead." I leaned into him and gave him a tiny kiss on the lingering contusion. Then I waited for the ceiling to fall on him. To my amazement, the red spot faded away. "I just wanted to make you feel a little better and thanks for today. It was fun. Well, at least parts of it were fun. I really enjoyed spending time with you. Let's hope we have better luck from here on out."

Hunter smiled at me and stood up and took my hand, kissing it lightly. I had never been around a man with such good manners and who treated me so nice. It was very refreshing. "The bumps and bruises were all worth it. Let's head out, shall we?"

We had a short drive to an upscale Italian restaurant where he maintained his perfect manners. I could tell he was doing his best to impress me and it sure as hell was working. During our meal, the conversation flowed easily and we covered a lot of ground. I asked him what he had planned for the weekend and when he told me, I dropped my fork. Oh FUCK!

"Well, this weekend, me and a couple of the roofers were invited to a cookout or something. Out in Skokie. I guess the old man wants to thank us for replacing his garage roof."

"Skokie? By any chance, was the name Harold Epstein?"

"Yeah, that's him. Why?"

"Oh my God. That's my Dad."

"Really! What a coincidence! How about it? We'll go together?" Then he paused. "Well, I mean, I don't want to make it seem like we are going to meet your parents, like we are in a relationship or something- um, that sounded awkward."

"No, no. I understand what you mean, and I think it would be a great idea. Even better, we can bring Kelly and Lindsey along to see your friends again. Seems like they really hit it off last time!"

"Well, we better keep them sober. I'd hate to see them start another game of strip poker in your parents' kitchen."

"Or worse." I was referring, of course, to the witchcraft induced ménage that was certain to play out unless I intervened. The next day I would have to do a little rewrite of events.

Later, Hunter took me home. We stood at my door and I invited him in, but to my surprise, he told me he had to be up early. He held me tight and gave me the sweetest kiss. My heart just melted and then we said goodnight.

Chapter Twelve

Going to a Garden Party

I woke up completely refreshed. The previous day's date with Hunter had worked out wonderfully and I couldn't wait to see him again. I was also relieved to have a possible solution to fixing the scheduled orgy at my parents' upcoming party. I made calls to both Lindsey and Kelly. The party at my mom and dad's house was going to be mandatory attendance for them. No excuses! I needed their talents to keep any stray roofers from getting snagged in any lingering magic, once I rewrote the script.

I had anguished over whether to just come up with a way to somehow cancel the party. I was afraid any cancellation would only delay the inevitable and most likely to a time when I would have no control over the events. I gave Lindsey's and Kelly's numbers to Hunter so that he could have the guys make their calls and invite the girls. My job was to be sure that they agreed to go.

The party was the next day. Luna and I both seemed to pace around, trying to decide what would be the best way to rewrite the story. It was nice having Luna around. I had become a witch and apparently she had become my classic witch's familiar, the black cat. I had been talking to her more, and that certainly had to help our relationship. It was a beautiful Friday afternoon and the weekend that I had been dreading was starting to look a little brighter. I owed that to Hunter.

My door opened and in came chaos. Lindsey and Kelly were laughing and joking, as if they were two school girls that had just been asked out to the prom.

"They called! Both of us got calls!" Lindsey said in a yelping high voice.

"Do you even know which one was which?" I asked.

"Leigh. You saw how freaking hot those guys are. You think it matters? I'd take any… or all."

"Well, I suppose you're right. Just as long as you keep them both focused on you. I am planning a little rewrite of the magic script, but just in case they feel compelled to do something crazy, you two need to stop them. I don't care how you do it."

"Great! So let's talk about this script. I want to set up some future dates with a roofer. So don't make it turn out badly for us." Lindsey's desperation was showing.

"Yes! Me, too. Let's write some steam, Leigh!" Kelly was nearly panting.

"Easy now, ladies, this has to be done very carefully. Almost anything can be taken very literally, and that is exactly how I got into this predicament to begin with."

I sat down at my desk and Luna joined me. Kelly and Lindsey looked over my shoulders as I turned on my monitor. "Now, here is the original piece where I was writing about Harry the werewolf and his evil woman. Harry's fate will be my Dad's fate, just as the woman's fate will be my Mother's. The werewolf hunters are already set to be played by the roofers. We'll start here, right before Harry is grabbed and tied up.

"If someone has to get tied up, can it be that roofer with the tattoos? I have some thoughts about that." Kelly spoke with sincerity as she chewed on one of her nails. Lindsey and I looked at her in disbelief.

"No! The idea is to prevent an erotic encounter, not create a BDSM dungeon in my parents' family room."

Lindsey was a little more helpful. "OK, write it so that we are all there at Harry's with our dates. God, I love saying that. With our dates. Anyway, so we all mingle about, and enjoy a good meal. The guys will be so focused on us they won't be able to pay attention to your parents."

"Good. Then, we can have Harry and his lady be totally and happily focused on each other. I really hope that I can change their fates, I just don't know if it will work. So please, at any sign of craziness, we all have to jump into action and clear the boys out of there. Just in case, I want to write in some silly, yet urgent reason for the boys to leave a little early."

"I got it. Just write in the guys were so happy to spend time with Lindsey and me that they begged to take us out for the evening, or something."

"Sounds good."

I tapped away on my keyboard and out came a couple of new paragraphs.

Beatrice had carefully set up her trap for Harry, but suddenly she felt something in her heart change. There was no way she could go through with any plan that would torment or hurt Harry. She realized that he was her mate. Her one true love. Harry felt the same way about her. The plans would change. She couldn't stop the werewolf hunters from coming over, so she decided that she would not disclose to them what Harry really was.

Meanwhile, the wolf hunters decided that perhaps they didn't want to go to Beatrice's lair alone and they brought along their beautiful girlfriends for company. The wolf hunters, Derek and Luke, were enamored with their new girlfriends and couldn't think of anything other than the women by their sides. What had once been planned as a trap by Beatrice to torture and humiliate the werewolf had become a friendly gathering and a time to celebrate newfound love.

"You know, I think that is probably going to be good enough. What do you think?" I looked back over my shoulders. Kelly and Lindsey nodded in agreement. With the new script in place and the backing of friends, I felt at ease about my parents' party.

The following morning went by without a hitch. Hunter arrived on time and was once again dressed smartly.

Kelly and Lindsey both called to say they were on their way with their rooftop escorts.

Our little caravan met up on the freeway and we headed for Skokie. We arrived at my parents' house by mid-afternoon.

I was happy to see my parents when we arrived. They were standing in the drive way as we pulled in. My Mother, as always, was dressed smartly in a light blue dress and matching blue heels. She wore her favorite white pearls with the matching earrings and bracelet. Her hairstyle had been unchanged since Ronald Reagan was president. There is not one time from my childhood that I can remember my Mom ever experimenting with her hair or her wardrobe. My Dad was wearing his typical embarrassing cookout clothing. Plaid shorts, a white button down shirt, and black dress shoes. Black dress shoes! His white socks were pulled to the maximum stretch level, nearly covering his pale bony knees. Ahhh... What can I say? It was good to see them.

The small crowd gathered on the driveway and after brief introductions, we all went into the somewhat tackily landscaped back yard. My parents loved lawn sculptures. The kind that were made out of poured cement and carefully arranged throughout the yard. Then, they were unceremoniously crapped on by every bird in the neighborhood.

All in all, things went great. My Dad ran the grill with Hunter as his assistant. The girls were busy getting to actually know their new friends. I was talking to my mother. The world was right again. As the afternoon wore on, my parents seemed to be getting a little cozy with each other and I patted myself on the back. It seems like being a witch is OK, once you get the hang of it.

Hunter and I took a walk through the yard. He commented, "So, is this like a pet cemetery or something?"

"No, my Dad owns a cement company and one of the things they make are these lawn ornaments. Angels, frogs, turtles, and fairies. When I was little, I would have nightmares after looking out here in the moonlight. They still creep me out."

"What's up with those monkeys? I've heard of the see no evil, hear no evil, speak no evil monkeys, but what happened there?" Hunter pointed to a cement log with three monkeys squatting along the top of it. Each cement monkey had a huge set of balls hanging below them and a very noticeable erection.

"Ha! It was from the shop. My Dad brought it home. I guess the guy that made it was quitting his job and thought it was funny. Just another thing that left scars on my young mind."

We walked back over to the gathering and I noticed my parents were missing. I led Hunter into the kitchen. He took me by the hands and looked me in the eye. For a minute I thought he might kiss me, until we heard a very odd sound. It was like a muffled sound coming from a person trying to talk with a mouth full of food.

We looked across the room and saw my Dad. He was on the other side of the kitchen island, leaning against it. His back was toward us and he didn't notice we were in the room.

"Dad? Are you OK? What's that noise?"

His head spun around and he had a shocked and embarrassed look on his face. My mother came up from behind the island. Her lipstick was smeared and her hair was tossed into disarray. Then I noticed it. Her blue dress had several gobs of thick, nasty, white stuff spattered on the front. You guessed it, love potion.

I stood there with my mouth hanging open as my mother very casually took a napkin and wiped her mouth off. "Hi, Leigh. Sorry, we didn't know you were in the kitchen." Some of the sticky liquid was on her chin. I started to gag. I turned away so that I wouldn't throw up.

"Oh. My. God."

"Leigh, your mother was just helping to tie my shoes!"

"Dad! You are wearing slip on shoes!"

I took Hunter by the hand and we walked briskly right out of the kitchen. "I'm sorry you had to see that, Hunter. I sure as hell hope *that* little blue dress makes it to the cleaner or the landfill."

"Ha! Well, I know one thing. I'm not about to accept a cigar from your Dad anytime soon!"

Hunter took me home and before we parted, he had to tell me something. "Leigh, like I said, I'm going into the Police Academy. I would like it very much if we could hang out a couple of times, at least until then. I'm not expecting anything, you know. I just thought it would be nice to spend some more time with you."

"I agree! Just so you know, I'm not dating anyone, or just out of a relationship, or any of that. Tell you what, we'll hang out, and I'll be there when you graduate at the top of your class to cheer for you. Then… we can go from there. Until then, I count today as our second date. I'm looking forward to a third." I winked at him and now that I had thrown my cards on the table about how I felt, I hoped our third date would rise to another level, just a bit.

It's good to be a witch. I've got the rest of summer ahead of me before I have to go back to teaching. I've got some crazy friends, parents that were in lust if not love, and a cat that has finally decided it's not all that bad to live with me. And best of all, the prospect of a great boyfriend. One that could actually measure up to my book boyfriends. Life is good.

For a short moment that is! I no sooner walked in the door and my cell phone started to buzz wildly. I looked at the caller ID and flipped my phone open.

"Hey girlie, how was the rest of your date? I saw that you and Lindsey made an early escape with your two beef cakes."

"What did you do to us? Leigh, this isn't funny. You have to fix the spell. Tweedle Dee and Tweedle Dumb seem to have lost all ability to think of anything but Lindsey and me. They don't even know their names anymore!"

"Oh, come on. It can't be *that* bad. So, they are a little fixated on you. You should appreciate it."

"Leigh! You have no idea. Luke was trying to tattoo my name on his chest with a nail. Thank God I was able to stop him. It's getting worse! We need you here, now. Help us, please!"

"I'll be right there." Like I said, things were looking good. I went to the living room to grab my purse. I stopped dead in my tracks. A large puff of smoke filled the center of the room, but that wasn't the strangest part. Luna walked out of the cloud of smoke and stood before me with a small scroll in her mouth. She dropped the scroll at my feet and greeted me with a loud "Meooow."

I picked up the scroll and broke the tiny seal that was placed in the middle. The wax seal was very old fashioned and had the number 1313 in the center. *What the hell is this?* I thought. I unrolled the scroll and began to read.

Ms. Epstein,

Congratulations on your new found powers. It has come to our attention that you have been practicing witchcraft as a non-union member. The practice of witchcraft is strictly forbidden in the mortal world without proper training and union membership.

You are hereby ordered to cease all magical use of any kind. You are ordered to appear in front of the Union Board immediately.

Please recite the following incantation out loud and you will be transported immediately to Union Headquarters. Please remember to bring a check book with you for any and all union dues along with any fines.

** Transportation Spell

Witches Local 1313, Take me there, Take me now. With ease and grace, This is how.

Seriously,

Esmeralda Jones

Command Secretary

Witches Local 1313

I read the letter twice to make sure I was reading it right! "Seriously?" I pulled my cellphone from my purse and called Kelly. "Hey, you're going to have to handle things there for a little bit without me."

"Leigh, you don't get it! We need you here- NOW! Everything is getting completely out of hand. The first time Lindsey and I were drunk, this time they are cursed. We don't want to take advantage of them like that. Luke and Derek are hot enough to begin with. I'm not sure Lindsey and I can fend them off when they're both so sweet and hot. They keep saying everything that a girl would ever want to hear, and their bodies are made for sin. Leigh! They are the *PERFECT* book boyfriends and we don't have the strength to say *NO*! Lindsey and I have talked about this. It's not that we don't want a night of amazing headboard banging, screaming like a banshee sex, we'd just rather not take full advantage of these guys when they're cursed! What if they come out of it and hate us for it? Right now, they don't even know their own names. It's like they live only to serve and please us. Did I mention they will do *ANYTHING* to prove it?"

I didn't know what to do. I knew that my friends needed me, but apparently I was being summoned by The Witches Local 1313. I'm still trying to wrap my brain around the fact that there is a Witches Union! Who would have thought? I can be pretty certain this is a group of people that I don't want to piss off, so I better do what I'm told. For now, anyway. . .

"Kelly, I'm sorry. I have an emergency here. I was just summoned, via my cat, to The Witches Local 1313 and before you ask, no… I'm not kidding. I don't have a choice! I have to go. I'll be there as soon as I can."

I quickly snapped my phone shut and threw it in my purse. I also double checked to make sure I had my checkbook with me as per the instructions in the letter. I sure as hell hoped this wasn't going to cost me an arm and a leg. Wait, scratch that thought! I hope it doesn't cost me a lot of money. The last thing I want is to return home missing a couple of limbs. That would seriously suck!

When I was finally ready, I bent over and picked Luna up. I figured if she had already met the witches, she

148

might as well go with me. Besides, I really didn't want to do this alone. I took one last deep breath and recited the transportation spell out loud. I should have been expecting the puff of smoke that surrounded me, but I wasn't. I immediately started choking and coughing before I felt myself being shifted from the comfort of my own home.

So much for life being good!

A Valentine's Surprise

Chapter 1

The day started out much like any other for Officer Adam Jennings. Riding with him in the front seat of his cruiser was his best friend and partner Jake Matthews. Being on patrol with Jake was one of his favorite places to be.

The only path that Adam ever saw for himself was that of a policeman. He liked helping people and this was the best way that he knew how. Sure he had to deal with the lowest of the low, but most of the citizens he interacted with were good people who just got off track every once in a while. He took his job seriously, but he still believed people should be given the benefit of the doubt. He firmly believed that most people tried hard to be good and do their best.

Adam was thankful he didn't live or work in a city with a high crime rate. He wanted the people in his community to feel safe. Whether they were home with their families, out and about running errands, or enjoying an evening on the town, their safety was important to him.

Adam had never been married, or even close to marriage. The only person he had to think about other than himself was his twenty-two year old sister, Jenny. When their parents died ten years earlier in a horrific car accident, Adam stepped up as a big brother to raise Jenny the best way that he could.

It wasn't always easy. He was fresh out of the police academy and knew nothing about raising a teenage girl, but he did his best and Jenny seemed to turn out all right. He was beyond grateful that she didn't rebel too much during her teen years. Adam didn't have the time or patience to deal with a bunch of teenage drama.

Jenny was a lot like Adam, in the respect that she didn't date a lot. There were the occasional boyfriends of course, but Adam never had to worry about killing them for hurting his sister.

Adam put the thought of any serious relationships on hold while he was raising Jenny. He didn't think it would be good for her to become attached to someone he was dating, especially if the relationship wasn't serious enough to lead to marriage. He tried to set a good example for her. The last thing he wanted was for his romantic exploits to make it back to his baby sister. Just the thought of it made him cringe.

Adam was no angel. He dated, but he did so discretely. He would only go out when he knew that Jenny had plans with her friends. He always made sure that whoever he went home with, knew up front that he would only be spending one night with them. Second dates were out of the question, because he *never* wanted anyone to get the wrong idea.

Dating had become easier now that Jenny was in college, but he still didn't find anyone that piqued his interest enough to want to settle down. Most of the women that he met were shallow, rude, and completely obtuse. The woman he would marry would be kind, compassionate, and witty. She would be independent, yet willing to stand beside him as an equal partner. He wasn't interested in anyone who was looking for a free ride. Women like that were to be avoided like the plague.

It was a quiet morning, as they traveled along their normal route. Adam and Jake had made a few traffic stops, but that was about it. Adam didn't mind quiet mornings, it meant the citizens of his sleepy town were safe and staying out of trouble. "I think it's time for our morning coffee stop," Jake said, breaking the comfortable silence.

"Sounds good," Adam replied, as they headed to the local convenience store. Adam noticed the empty parking lot, as they slowly exited the car and closed the doors. He took the lead, as he and Jake entered the store. There was nothing normal about what was happening, as Adam stepped inside.

Before he could react to what he saw, he heard a loud BANG and was knocked backward by an excessive force. He felt a burning in his shoulder, chest, and lungs. He yelled out in pain, as he reached for his shoulder.

He was shocked when he pulled his hand back, it was warm, and wet, and covered with blood. The pain took his breath away and he began fighting for air as he collapsed to the floor. Adam heard two more shots ring out. The only thing he could think of was Jake. He prayed that his partner wasn't hit.

Adam could hear the sirens in the distance. Jake knelt beside him yelling his name. He tried to focus on what Jake was saying, but the pain was too much. Thoughts of Jenny ran through his mind. He always thought he would have a chance to say goodbye to her. "Look after Jenny," he mumbled to Jake. The darkness kept pulling him under, as he fought to keep his eyes opened. Soon the darkness offered a beautiful respite from the pain that could no longer be denied.

Conjuring Darkness

Chapter 1

Lexi quickly glanced in the mirror hanging on the wall. It was more of a habit than anything, much like the halfhearted effort she took to run her fingers through her shoulder length auburn hair before she headed out the door. Just like every day before, she deftly gathered it in a quick ponytail, shouldered her bag and grabbed her keys.

Before opening the door, she tapped the old gold ring that she wore on the small finger of her left hand against the brass door knob. The ring was the only thing she owned that had been her mother's and she never took it off. After she made a few more clinking sounds, a fuzzy black cat came bounding down the stairs. A series of rapid thumps resonated in the old house. They were the telltale signs of a very spoiled and very portly feline.

In a cartoon-like scene, the cat's back legs slipped, as it skidded across the dark wooden floorboards and around the corner. The cat gained traction and speed, as it bolted across the faux Persian runner and then it came to an abrupt stop. The cat looked at Lexi with a wide eyed stare, as if it were trying to hypnotize Lexi with its bright yellow eyes. The cat sang out a single "meow," pleading to come along for the day. "Hello there, Allie cat. OK fine, you can come along, you bowling ball with a tail." Together they walked out the front door.

The familiar squeaks from the worn wooden boards on the front porch comforted Lexi. She had been living in the old Victorian style farmhouse for just over a year. The realty agent was more than optimistic when he described it as a piece of history, a fixer-upper, and a handyman's dream. He had told her that it was a steal at the price and anyone with a little gumption could turn this diamond-in-the-rough into a polished gem.

Lexi learned later that the do-it-yourself old house shows on television were just as misleading as the agent had been. Anything that exceeded Lexi's skill level and budget had to wait. Still, Lexi was proud of her creativity and the improvements that she had accomplished.

When her sister saw pictures of the place, she thought it was a style created by accident. Her actual words were, "It looks like a bargain-mart truck crashed into a flea market. Then some drunken elves picked up the debris and decided to throw it all over your house, Lexi!"

Lexi smiled, as she remembered Kate's voice. It had been so long since she had seen her and she wondered how Kate was handling the grief of losing her husband Kurt two years ago. As she opened the door to let Allie into the truck, she looked up into the large tree that reached a long arm toward her bedroom window. There was an owl in that tree the night before and Lexi recalled how it looked then, as she looked out her bedroom window. She had seen the owl as a horned silhouette against the full moon. It chanted a few lonely notes into the night and then it sat still and silent, as if it were gazing back at Lexi.

As she replayed the scene in her head, she felt a chilly uneasiness once again and wondered why the owl seemed to bother her. *Well, it's not there now. Aren't owls an omen for something? An ancient symbol for sure. Got to remember to ask Kate about it the next time we talk.* To Lexi, things like omens were simply trivia topics and they held no useful purpose, other than to spur one's curiosity.

Lexi's old truck bounced and jolted its way down the deserted highway toward town. Allie stretched herself across the faded and cracked dashboard to soak in the morning sun.

156

Lexi loved driving across the open plain toward the mountains on the horizon. After so many years of feeling stifled by the crowded and humid east coast, this new open place renewed her thirst for adventure.

Southwest Montana was a spotless sheet of paper, just waiting for her to write her own future. The last thing she wanted was to be confined into one of the expected roles of the citizens in the sprawling cities. To have had accepted a fate like that, would have killed her very soul. Lexi thought that too many people were already forced to wade through a pool of hypocrisy in order to survive.

For some people, picking up and moving cross country into a new life might be considered a fool's journey, but for Lexi it was a purposeful step taken into the unknown. Montana was one of those places where she felt a person could be propelled into anything. As soon as she had received her bachelor's degree, she found a little dusty corner bookstore for sale on an online listing and she bought it, sight unseen. The two made their epic journey from Virginia to Montana a year prior. The ever faithful Allie was a good listener, when it came to Lexi's singing and travel commentary.

An entire year had gone by and Lexi started to feel something that was a bit unexpected, boredom. That first year was chaotic and busy, but Lexi relished in the challenge, as she took on the repairs to her house and opened her store. Now that her life had finally settled into a routine, she found herself missing the hectic, yet satisfying feeling she got from conquering each new task. Lexi longed for something truly exciting and adventurous to happen to her. It seemed to Lexi that perhaps the only romance and adventure that she could expect, would probably come from between the covers of her cherished novels.

Lexi pulled up to the curb and parked in front of her store. The large glass windows displayed an array of carefully selected new books. She had arranged some hiking guides, a few local western books and a very visible display of books about fly fishing. In a town like this, you had to know who the paying customers were, if you expected to keep the lights on. The mountains, parks, and blue ribbon trout streams in the area, attracted exactly the type of people Lexi wanted to get through her door. Large red letters prominently showed the name "THE LEXICON, Books and More, Lexi Salenko, owner."

She followed her usual sequence of turning on the lights, radio and computer. Allie made a half-hearted attempt to be on mouse patrol, as she strolled between the display racks. Once the cat felt satisfied that she had reasonably completed her duties, she transformed into a fluffy black ball on a bookshelf.

The store was small, but it had some additional space in a loft section that was accessible by ornate wrought iron spiral stairs. The upper area made a cozy place for various collectable antique books that sold very well. The old, red brick walls of the store were decorated with framed poster art that was inspired by classic literature. Lexi looked around and felt satisfied with the niche she had created for herself in Montana, even though it depleted the remaining balance of the trust fund left to her by her parents.

The front door swung open and rang a string of small bells that dangled from the frame. A red haired, green eyed Marcie bounced to the register. Marcie's daily arrival always brought a smile to Lexi. She leaned as far over the counter as she could, letting her long, loose red curls fall forward. She planted a wet kiss on Lexi and boisterously laughed at Lexi's reaction. "What the hell! Marcie?"

"Just checking. I guess you're straight after all, Lex. I was kind of hoping the rumors were true. I mean if you weren't, then I would have a bunch of questions for you." Marcie laughed again and walked toward the undisturbed Allie.

"What!" Lexi cawed. "So now, who was behind *this* rumor?"

Marcie continued to stroke Allie's silky black coat and turned to Lexi. "Who knows? Just look at what other people see when they look at you. You're never seen with a guy, even though you are hot as hell. You have this mysterious foreign British accent. You have your own business and your own house. Face it, you intimidate the guys around here. So of course, rather than just admitting that they are substandard excuses for men, they chose to run their big stupid mouths. Of course, that tire changing incident probably has something to do with it also. Remember the way you went all ninja on that guy?" Marcie said, as she roared with laughter.

"How could I forget? I'm sure I'm legendary for my man-hating skills now."

"You pepper sprayed him Lex, and kicked his junk all the way to Canada! Legendary is a good word. Legendary ball buster!"

Lexi remembered the incident that played out shortly after her arrival in town. Her truck had a flat tire and she found herself stranded on a dark country road. The only light came from the flashlight she had laid on the ground. A house was nearby, but was dark and quiet and Lexi didn't think this job required any help. While she was busy working to jack the vehicle up, a large shadowy man appeared next to her. He picked up the four way lug wrench that Lexi had left on the ground next to her.

"You look like you could use a man right about now, little lady" he said. Lexi turned and was shocked by the menacing appearance of him holding the lug wrench. Instinctively, the self-defense training her bother-in-law Kurt had given her, kicked in. She leaned back on one hand, balancing herself on the heel of her bent leg. She lifted her other leg and spun around in a swift sweeping semicircle. Her foot hit the back of his ankle with full force.

The stranger's feet flew out from under him, as he landed with a grunt. Before he could utter a single curse, Lexi had drawn a canister of pepper spray from her bag and was dousing him, as if she were trying to kill a deadly spider with a can of bug spray. The coup-de-grace was a lightning quick kick to his crotch. In a scene only likely to be watched on a zombie apocalypse movie, a woman in an ankle length nightgown ran out of the house and down the drive toward Lexi. As she neared the car, Lexi noticed the green, pasty skin of her face. There was a chorus of children's screams that followed her like a flock of unseen harpies. They were pleading and begging for his life.

It became clear to Lexi that the frightening woman had been attempting some sort of badly needed facial, but was interrupted by the commotion outside. She screamed at Lexi and cursed her, as if she were a female demon that she was trying to compel back to hell. The zombie bride gathered her huddled, sobbing mass of a crushed husband and led him back to the house.

She only turned back once to utter some additional curses, to ensure the damnation of Lexi the demon. The children's pleas had become curses equally as abusive as their mother's. Her last fading sounds were the orders she screamed at her brood on the porch, as she ushered them into the house.

"But don't feel too bad," Marcie continued. "I heard that she threatened him a few times since then. I guess she dragged him out of a bar one night and told him she was going to have that bookstore bitch go crazy on him! So you've got all that going for you, Lex."

"Don't worry about me, Marcie. I certainly don't need a man to get through life, and to be honest, I don't find them all that entertaining. Take a look at that last date you set me up on. He took me to Mario's, that trendy new Italian bistro. That was fine, except when the waiter asked if we wanted a cocktail, he started doing tequila shots. *TEQUILA SHOTS* Marcie! Who does that at a romantic upscale restaurant? He started to puke for Pete's sake. I don't think he ever noticed that I got up and walked out. Thanks, by the way, for picking me up that night."

"What are friends for? The list of available guys around here is pretty short. There is one guy you could try out, but from the stories I've heard… well, let's just say that if you want to get a little from him, you might as well just ask for an apology up front and be done with it. Save yourself two minutes of disappointment, if you know what I mean. So I guess that just leaves me, baby!" Marcie gave Lexi a quick kiss on her cheek.

"Oh and don't forget yoga class tonight! Be there or die, or something." Marcie laughed and headed for the door. Lexi whipped Marcie on her ass with a nearby cat toy wand, as she walked away. "If I decide to switch teams, you are first on my list, Marcie." Lexi playfully went along with the theme of her joke, and she watched as Marcie blushed and bounced out the door. "Crazy kid." Lexi whispered.

Allie jumped down from her perch and leapt up onto the counter. Her tail wrapped around Lexi's arm, trying to elicit a gift of treats. Lexi stroked Allie Cat's furry head. "Marcie knows I am not looking for anything, right? We're good," she thought to herself. *She knows that trust is really hard for me to grant to anyone. After all, she is one person I have allowed myself to open up to, so I know she gets it. When it comes to love, I may not have any experience or know what to look for, but I sure as hell know what I DON'T want. I've seen plenty of examples of that misery. Thank God for Marcie, even a loner like me, needs a best friend like her.*

Lexi glanced in the mirror behind the display case. She felt comfortable with how she looked. She didn't often wear make-up or spend too much time with her long locks. She wasn't self-conscious of her body. She had always had a petite frame, but not bony. She had ample sized breasts and a cute face. The feature she admired most was her emerald green eyes, because they looked exactly like her mother's. Her only complaint was that at 5'2", she wished she could be a little taller. Lexi never wanted to be a super-model anyway. She preferred her cute rounded features, to the scary sunken faces on those high cheek-boned, collagen lipped things that graced the covers of magazines. She was a little embarrassed when she received compliments, but at least it fueled her self-esteem and she was getting better at accepting them.

The bells on the door announced a visitor and Lexi turned to see who was coming in. She had seen the delivery man a hundred times before and she always wondered the same thing. He seemed much too old the way he huffed and puffed from address to address. He had the look of someone who wished they were doing something else. Maybe it was retirement he looked forward to. Maybe he resented his superiors that were old enough to be his grandchildren. The old man placed a large, brightly colored envelope onto the counter and held up a small palm sized piece of technology. After he punched in some numbers, he held the device out to Lexi for an electronic signature. Lexi noticed that the envelope had been badly torn and taped together. It had black smudge marks that looked like it had been run through broken machinery and then left on a road to be run over by every delivery truck that was able to move.

A good opportunity for sarcasm was never wasted by Lexi, "Do you normally destroy the packages before delivering them, or is that an extra charge?"

"Sorry ma'am. That's just the way it came to me. You have to sign for it. If anything is damaged, you have to claim it online."

"I bet it's a real handy user-friendly process too." Lexi mumbled, as she looked at the envelope in front of her, curious to see what this could be.

She thought briefly about the delivery man again, as his truck careened around the corner and down the street. She turned her attention to the badly damaged package. *What is this?* She thought. *The senders name is Kate, but why is this coming from an address in Israel? That's how lives are completely turned upside down by mailmen and delivery people, complete strangers going about their business, never knowing what they have left behind in their wake. This could be the door to adventure or to a nightmare.*

She yanked the thick paper tab that ripped a thin plastic ribbon from the envelope. Lexi reached into the newly ripped opening and fished out a handwritten letter, that had been largely destroyed by what she imagined was some mechanical T-Rex that was on a strict diet of important packages. Along with the letter, there was an index card that had a couple of phone numbers and a brass key taped to the back.

Hah! The Key to adventure! Lexi set the letter down in front of her and saw that it looked like her sister's familiar neat handwriting, but the lines seemed skewed. *Kate would never have skewed her lines like that, unless she was in a hurry.* Lexi flattened it out on the counter and began to read. The mangling machine had damaged the letter so badly, that Lexi had a difficult time making out all of the words. Some areas were completely illegible and were at best partial sentences.

Lexi

I hate to ask you this, but I really have no choice. Right now I'm in Haifa Israel visiting Dr. Jakub Meier, but I am on my way to Turkey soon to do some research at the Gobekli Tepe site. I need some help. I know you are settled in your new place and very busy, but you are the only one I can trust. I need you to go back to our place in Arlington. The key that you have received came off of my key chain and it is for the drawer in Kurt's old desk at the house. In there, is a notebook that has the contact information and the instructions on how to get a hold of a man named Kidd. Kurt had once told me he is the only person that he could trust outside of the country. He said if any of us ever got into something serious, to get a hold of Kidd. (This

*part was badly damaged and unreadable)
Mr. Kidd will help you.*

*Go into the safe in my bedroom closet.
I had it set to the same numbers as
ALWAYS. Inside, there is a very old
coin. That is the thing I need you to
bring. Do not let anyone see it. Don't
let anyone know you have it. Take as
much cash out of the safe as you need.*

*That coin is (unreadable) and you need
to (unreadable) Haifa Israel.*

*Once you get a hold of Mr. Kidd, you
need to have him escort you with the
coin (unreadable). We cannot use our
cell phones. Remember what Kurt told us
about cell phones?*

*Kidd. To get ahold of Mr. Kidd. You can
only call him from the phone on Kurt's
old desk, because it is secure. Use the
instructions that Kurt left in case we
ever needed help. Tell him that Kurt
said it was time to return a favor.
Then (unreadable)*

Book a flight (unreadable)

*That old coin is actually a
(unreadable)*

Love you, Sis

"Christ! Really Kate? You can't
call? Were you drunk or asleep when you
wrote this?" Lexi shouted loud enough
to call Allie to attention and then she
looked at the letter again to check the

date. Lexi's heart started to race, when she realized that this letter had been written six weeks ago. She grabbed her cell phone and immediately dialed Kate's cell. A dozen attempts only brought the same response, "please leave a message after the tone."

Made in the USA
Middletown, DE
22 February 2015